"I've made up my mind. Everything's settled," she muttered to herself.

A voice, flavored with hints of sunny Italy and laced with a forbidding undercurrent of steel, announced softly, "Everything is indeed settled, Cassandra."

Dismayed, Cassandra gaped as Benedict Constantino stepped into the room from the balcony.

"But not," he continued, "quite the way you suppose. Far from it, in fact."

Clearly he'd listened in on every word of her conversation with Trish and didn't like it one little bit.

"So, there is a baby on the way," he said conversationally. "How do you propose we deal with this unexpected turn of events?"

"*We* don't. This isn't your problem, Benedict," she replied.

"A child is never a problem. But if I am the father, then it most assuredly becomes my concern. *Is* this baby mine, Cassandra?"

"It's yours."

"Then our next move is clear enough. We shall be married."

EXPECTING!

She's sexy,
successful...
and
PREGNANT!

Relax and enjoy our fabulous series about
couples whose passion ends in
pregnancies...sometimes unexpected!
Of course, the birth of a baby is always a
joyful event, and we can guarantee that our
characters will become wonderful moms
and dads—but what happened in
those nine months before?

Share the surprises, emotions, drama and
suspense as our parents-to-be come to terms
with the prospect of bringing a new baby
into the world. All will discover that the
business of making babies brings with it
the most special love of all....

Coming soon:

Their Secret Baby
by Kate Walker
#2432

His Pregnancy Ultimatum
by Helen Bianchin
#2433

Delivered only by Harlequin Presents®

Catherine Spencer

CONSTANTINO'S PREGNANT BRIDE

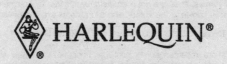

HARLEQUIN®

TORONTO • NEW YORK • LONDON
AMSTERDAM • PARIS • SYDNEY • HAMBURG
STOCKHOLM • ATHENS • TOKYO • MILAN • MADRID
PRAGUE • WARSAW • BUDAPEST • AUCKLAND

ISBN 0-373-12423-6

CONSTANTINO'S PREGNANT BRIDE

First North American Publication 2004.

Copyright © 2003 by Kathy Garner.

This edition published by arrangement with Harlequin Books S.A.

® and TM are trademarks of the publisher. Trademarks indicated with ® are registered in the United States Patent and Trademark Office, the Canadian Trade Marks Office and in other countries.

www.eHarlequin.com

Printed in U.S.A.

CHAPTER ONE

CASSANDRA WILDE stepped out of the elevator of the office complex where her company was located, and pushed open the heavy plate-glass doors of Ariel Enterprises. Immediately, the discreet hum of success surrounded her, from the restrained and melodic chime of the phone, to the quiet conversation of clients in the open lounge to the left of the reception area.

Normally, she'd have stopped to acknowledge familiar faces, and make sure people visiting for the first time were being well looked after. But not today. There was nothing "normal" about today.

"Oh, Cassie!" Meghan called out as she passed her personal assistant's desk. "There's a visitor—"

But Cassie merely shook her head and kept on going until she was safely inside the sanctuary of her own office. Then, and only then, did her tight, professional smile slip into obscurity, washed away by yet another fit of soundless, hopeless weeping.

Leaning against the closed door, she stared through her tears at the blurred image before her. Sunlight bounced in rainbow prisms through the floor-to-ceiling windows and fell across the pale gray carpet in a swath of gold. It turned her rich mahogany desk into a cube of iridescent ruby, and studded the silver frame holding a photograph of her late mother with shimmering ersatz diamonds.

One end of the sliding windows stood open a foot or two. Outside, on the small balcony, a planter of freesias dispersed their delicate scent on the warm March breeze wafting into the room. From fourteen floors below, the muted din of street traffic merged with the raucous shriek of seagulls soaring under the blue bowl of the sky.

It was a perfect spring day in San Francisco. And one of the bleakest Cassie had known in all her twenty-seven years. But crying about it would do no one any good, nor would it change her situation, so making a real effort to control herself, she stepped away from the door.

She needed to calm down. Confront matters head-on. Adjust her plans for the future which, all at once, had changed shape dramatically. She needed to *focus!*

But her thoughts kept harking back to a chance meeting with a man who lingered in her thoughts, as sharply defined as if she'd last seen him just yesterday; as if it had been only last night that he'd taken her in his arms and taught her how pale and insignificant her previous sexual encounters with men had been.

How slender the coincidence which had brought them together. And yet, how fatally life-altering!

It had begun innocently enough, early the previous summer. She and Patricia Farrell, her best friend since Grade Two and, for the last four years, her business partner, had driven up to the Napa Valley to confer with Nuncio Zanetti, a valued client and owner of one of California's most acclaimed wineries. Twice a year, he rewarded his employees with a dinner cruise on *The Ariel,* the ninety-six-foot motor yacht which she and Trish had bought at the beginning of their working relationship.

Nuncio was a generous man who enjoyed spending money and whose tastes ran to the extravagant. But he was also demanding, and expected of others the same attention to detail he brought to his own endeavors. Choreographing one of his social events entailed months of meticulous organization, an iron-clad guarantee that every clause in his contract would be honored, and a willingness, particularly on Cassie's part, to take the time to consult with him in person, whenever he requested, even if it was only to confirm that plans were moving ahead smoothly and according to the blueprint they'd drawn up together.

That particular sun-filled day, when she and Trish had arrived to finalize arrangements for his Midsummer Night's cruise, he introduced them to Benedict Constantino. A childhood friend of Nuncio's, Benedict told them he now lived mostly in New York from where he oversaw international distribution of his family's citrus products.

"Most especially the bergamot," he told them, when they asked. "It grows only in a very small area of southern Italy, which makes it a rare commodity worldwide. You're probably familiar with its use in fine perfumes, but what you might not be aware of is that, among its other applications, it's of great value to the pharmaceutical industry."

Later, when the discussion turned to living in New York, he'd smiled at Cassie with particular warmth, and said, "I find the energy of the city exciting, but I can see many advantages to dividing my time between there and the west coast. California, I suddenly discover, holds unsuspected attractions, also."

Thoroughly captivated by his European charm and sophistication, Cassie and Trish had been easily persuaded to join both men for lunch in the winery's beautiful private garden, once the business of the day was concluded.

They'd spent a delightful three hours, lingering over

scallop ceviche and the sparkling red wine for which the Zanetti vineyard was famous, and if Cassie had thought her imagination was working overtime in believing the handsome stranger had shown more than a passing interest in her, she certainly learned differently, the next time they happened to meet.

An imperious rap at her office door brought a swift end to her reminiscing. A second later, Trish stepped into the room, her brow furrowed with concern. "Cassie? I saw you come in just now and you didn't look…quite right. Is everything okay?"

For a few brief moments, Cassie had managed if not to forget the predicament facing her, then at least to relegate it to the sidelines. But at her friend's question, it came roaring back to the forefront of her mind, and the waterworks started up all over again, gushing forth with renewed vigor.

Trish let out a horrified gasp, promptly shut the door before the ragged sobs reached the ears of the people in the outer office, and whispered, "Cass, you're scaring me! The last time I saw you this upset was at your mom's funeral, and the time before that was when we were six and went to see the movie *Bambi*."

"Well, crying's the last thing in the world I planned to do right now," Cassie wailed, lurching behind the desk and flopping down in her chair. But the irony implicit in the word "planned" sent her already raging hormones into overdrive and produced another round of humiliating tears.

Trish perched on the arm of the chair, stroked Cassie's hair away from her forehead, and begged, "Talk to me! Whatever the problem is, we'll handle it together, the way we always do."

"Not this time," Cassie sniffed, so awash in self-pity,

regret and morning sickness that she didn't care if she lived or died. "This is a mess entirely of my own making."

"It can't be that bad."

"It's worse than bad. It's...inexcusable. Shameful."

"Shameful?" Trish rolled the word around her palate as if it were a morsel of unfamiliar food, and when she spoke again, there was a note of amusement in her voice. "Hey, I know you had an outside appointment this morning and that you were perfectly fine before that, so what happened between the time you left here and the time you came back again, that you now have reason to feel ashamed? Did you lose one our biggest accounts? Make such a colossal miscalculation on a quote that we're headed for bankruptcy?"

"No. The company's never been more solidly in the black. It's my personal life that's falling apart." Aware of the thread of anxiety underlying Trish's attempt to treat the situation lightly, Cassie plucked a tissue from the box at her elbow and made a heroic effort to pull herself together.

She blew her nose and deciding she might just as well come straight to the point since dancing around the subject would do nothing to lessen its impact, said bluntly, "My appointment this morning had nothing to do with business. I went to see a doctor. An obstetrician." She waited a second to let the significance of that sink in, then finished off with the obvious. "I'm pregnant."

"Pregnant? No, you're not!" Trish scoffed. "You never find time for a steady relationship with anyone, and you're definitely not the one-night stand type."

Cassie didn't answer. Couldn't, if truth be told, because she was too embarrassed even to look her friend in the eye. But her silence spoke revealing volumes and Trish was too astute to miss their meaning.

Her mouth fell open. "Good grief, you did! *Cassandra!* You had a one-night stand!"

"Uh-huh." Cassie swallowed. "And that's not the worst of it. There's more."

But the rest—the part which hadn't struck Cassie as too terrible while she was in the doctor's office, but which had grown more foreboding with every passing minute since—went ignored. Trish was still reeling, too shell-shocked from what she'd already learned, to cope with "more." "Are you absolutely sure—that you're pregnant, I mean?"

"I'm sure."

You're a good ten weeks along, the obstetrician had confirmed. *With proper care and if you're very lucky, you'll be hanging an extra stocking from the mantel next Christmas.*

If you're very lucky...

"But—" Trish paused, clearly trying to step as delicately as possible through the minefield suddenly confronting her "—who's the father?"

Cassie opened her mouth to reply, but fear closed her throat. *What if the pregnancy didn't go well? If the complication the doctor suspected did, in fact, occur?*

"Cass?" As the silence lengthened, Trish draped her arm around Cassie's shoulders. "You *do* know who he is, don't you?"

Outraged, Cassie spluttered, "Well, of course I do! I might be all kinds of a fool, but I'm not a slut!"

"Honey, I never meant to suggest you were! But if you were coerced..." Trish's voice sank to a near whisper, as if loath to put into words the ugly suspicion suddenly tainting her thoughts. "If you didn't know the man…if he forced you….

"I wasn't raped, if that's what you're afraid of," Cassie said hurriedly. "I knew the man, and I was…more than willing."

Embarrassingly enthusiastic, in fact! Depressingly eager!

"So he has a name." Less a statement than a question, the remark hung in the air, stubbornly waiting to be acknowledged.

On a sigh of defeat, Cassie wiped a hand over her face. "Yes, he has a name. It's…Benedict Constantino."

She muttered the name furtively, as if she were afraid the walls had ears. Trish, though, exercised no such discretion. "Benedict Constantino?" she squealed, loudly enough to send the seagull perched on the balcony railing fluttering away in alarm. *"Benedict Constantino?"*

"Broadcast it to the whole world while you're at it, why don't you?" Cassie said peevishly, too nauseated to care that she was making a rare exhibition of herself.

Immediately contrite, Trish said, "I'm sorry, I really am. But if you'd asked me to guess who in the world might have lured you into his bed, for a one-night stand of all things, Benedict Constantino's is the last name I'd have chosen. He's so aloofly correct. So…gorgeously unattainable."

Hardly words to describe him the last time she'd seen him, Cassie thought, turning hot inside even all these months later, at the fresh onslaught of memory. *That* night, the man she'd previously known only as the charming friend of a business acquaintance had shown himself capable of blistering passion, and all without benefit of anything as mundane as a bed!

Trish was regarding her as if she'd suddenly sprouted two heads. "How did it…happen?"

"Well, how do you think?" Cassie snapped. "He might be rich, powerful and beautiful, but he still puts his pants on one leg at a time, just like any other man."

"And takes them off the same way, it would seem, but I wasn't asking about *that*," Trish said. "We might have been friends for a lifetime, but that hardly entitles me to poke my nose into every last intimate detail affecting your life. What I meant was, how did you happen to run into him again? It's not as if he lives down the street, after all. New York's not exactly next door to San Francisco."

"He flew out for Nuncio Zanetti's New Year's Eve party."

"New Year's…?" Trish's eyes grew big as saucers, as awareness dawned. "Oh! *Oh! That* night!"

"Yes, that night," Cassie echoed glumly.

"So it really was a spur of the moment fling. If it hadn't been that one of our staff got sick and couldn't work the New Year's Eve cruise, you'd probably have spent the night watching TV at home. Instead, you stepped in to cover her absence, ran into Benedict again, and—"

"And while the rest of the guests on board welcomed the New Year in traditional style, Benedict and I celebrated less conventionally, and I was left with a gift that'll keep on giving for the rest of my life!" The tears began again, swamping her voice. "I feel like such an idiot!"

Trish pushed the box of tissues closer. "Come on, Cassie, this isn't like you!" she said bracingly. "You've never been the type to fold under pressure. You don't weep and wail, you cope."

"Not this time, I don't!"

"Of course you do! You're not the first woman to find herself facing an unplanned pregnancy, and you won't be the last. If you absolutely feel a baby's more than you can handle, you do have other options. There's adoption and…abortion."

"As if I'd even consider either one!" Cassie wailed, pressing protective hands over her womb and wondering if she was destined to weep her way through the next six and a half months.

"Then why the emotional meltdown? Is it Benedict? Has he refused to acknowledge that the baby's his?"

Hearing the mixture of confusion and exasperation in her friend's voice, Cassie made a monumental effort to bring her runaway emotions to heel. "No, it's not about Benedict!" she said, which wasn't true, because of course it was partly about him. But she'd had ten weeks to adjust to the fact that while she hadn't been able to forget him or the circumstances which had led to their making love, he'd clearly had no trouble wiping all memory of the event, and her, clean out of his mind. "It's…my mother."

"Oh, honey!" Trish's voice softened. "I know how much you miss her, and you must find it especially painful at a time like this, but you're not alone. You have me and Ian, and while I know we'll never fill Nancy's shoes, you really can count on us to be there for you."

"It's not that, either. It's…" Another flood of tears welled up, threatening to drown her. Swallowing, she forced them down again. "It's that the baby's due on…October the eighth."

Trish sucked in a sympathetic breath. "Your mom's birthday?"

"Mmm-hmm. I don't know why it should upset me

so much. If anything, it ought to make me feel better—as if Mom's somehow watching over me. As if she's giving me the gift of another life, to make up for losing her.'' Cassie mopped her eyes one last time, and managed a smile at the expression on her friend's face. ''Stop looking at me as if I've lost my mind! Pregnant women are allowed to be fanciful. It goes with the territory.''

''Maybe. But you've been under a lot of stress lately, what with business heating up as the summer approaches, and now this.'' Trish regarded her doubtfully. ''Maybe you should forget work, and take a few days off. Maybe arrange to meet Benedict somewhere, and both of you come to terms with this new development. How do you think he'll take the news?''

''He won't. I don't plan to tell him.''

''Not tell him? But he has a right to know, Cassie! It's his child, as well, and two parents are almost always better than just one.''

''It didn't hurt me, growing up without a father.''

''Oh, yes, it did. You just learned at an early age not to let it show. But there's no reason to saddle this baby with more of the same. Although I don't pretend to know him well, Benedict Constantino strikes me as the honorable type—the kind of man who'd face up to his mistakes and do the right thing.''

''He wasn't too concerned with doing the right thing when he had sex with me on New Year's Eve.''

''At risk of stating the obvious, it takes two, Cass, and let me remind you that, by your admission, you didn't exactly rebuff him.''

''No, I didn't,'' Cassie admitted, not so far gone in self-pity that she'd delude herself on that score. ''But it was his fault. He was just too…seductive for me to say 'no.'"

Trish grinned. "I can see how that might happen. He gives new depth and meaning to the term, *tall, dark and handsome,* and all I can say is that between his genes and yours, you'll have made a beautiful baby."

Beautiful, yes. Provided…

"And one he'd want to acknowledge, even if it turned out to be homely as a board fence. You really do have to let him know, Cass."

So they were back to that again, were they! "I'm not telling him," Cassie said flatly, "and neither are you. Let me be very clear on this, Patricia! What I've just told you remains in this room."

"Well, I'm not about to take out a full page ad in *The San Francisco Chronicle,* if that's what you're afraid of, but I surely don't have to point out that this isn't the kind of secret you can keep indefinitely."

"This is my first baby. I probably won't show that much."

"Possibly not. But the next time Benedict shows up in town, which likely will be for Nuncio's Midsummer Night's party this June, you'll be a good six months along, my dear, and sticking out in front enough that there'll be no hiding the fact that you are, as they say in polite society, with child. So how do you plan to handle that?"

"I'll take a vacation and leave you to deal with Nuncio."

"I'm in charge of catering, not marketing and PR. That's your department, Cassie."

"Then I'll take care of things over the phone or by e-mail."

"You're dreaming! Nuncio will be expecting the personal, hands-on approach he's always received from you, and given the size of his account with us, you can't afford to disappoint him. This isn't just about you anymore, you know. You have a child's future to think of, and babies don't come cheap these days.''

"For heaven's sake, Trish, I'm not exactly short of money!''

"You're not exactly worth millions, either,'' Trish said, ''so if you're determined to go the parenting route alone, you'd better be willing to cater to the likes of Signor Zanetti, because I'm here to tell you, you're going to be glad of accounts like his when it comes time to think about medical expenses, private schools, orthodontics, riding lessons, and all the other extras you'll want to lavish on this child.''

"Fine,'' Cassie said, too overwhelmed by the possible problems facing her in the next few months to worry about what might happen years from now. "Then I'll have all the arrangements nailed down by the beginning of May which is only six weeks away. I won't be showing then, nor will I be in any danger of accidentally running into Benedict.''

"And how long do you think you can keep this secret?''

"Until enough time has passed that no one's going to question when or by whom I became pregnant.''

Trish glanced at her watch and rolled her eyes. "You're dreaming!'' she said again. "If it weren't that I'm running late for a meeting with a supplier, I'd stay and point out the folly of such thinking, but don't for a moment think I'm leaving it at that. The subject is by no means closed.''

"Oh, yes, it is,'' Cassie said, leaning back in her chair and pressing the heels of her hands against her eyes as the door swung shut behind her friend. "I've made up my mind. Everything's settled."

Scarcely had she spoken though, when she sensed, rather than saw or heard, that she was not alone, after all. A trembling heartbeat later, she knew it for certain as a voice seasoned with dark, rich mocha, flavored with hints of sunny Italy, and laced with a forbidding undercurrent of steel, announced softly, "Everything is indeed settled, Cassandra."

Dismayed, she dropped her hands and gaped in stunned amazement as Benedict Constantino stepped into the room through the partially open glass door leading from the balcony.

"But not," he continued, his long legs carrying him across the carpet with frighteningly stealthy speed, "quite the way you suppose. Far from it, in fact."

Clearly, he'd listened in on every word of her conversation with Trish. Clearly, he'd understood the exact context of what he'd heard and didn't like it one little bit. A complete stranger lacking the usual complement of brain cells could have taken one look at his face, and recognized immediately that he was furious and in no mood to play games.

But Cassie, sitting there as if she'd been poleaxed, paid no heed to the evidence staring her in the face, and instead climbed on her woefully inappropriate high horse and said haughtily, "I don't know what you're talking about, but I *would* like to know how you managed to break into my office. You have exactly one minute to explain yourself, and then I'm calling Security."

"Be silent!" he commanded, oozing contempt. "You will call no one!"

She'd been intimate with him. He'd seen her with her

breasts exposed. With her skirt drawn up around her waist, and her legs spread wide to accommodate him.

He'd touched her most private flesh. He'd known how hungry for him she'd been. How willing. She'd gazed in awe at the power of his arousal. Cradled its pulsing weight in her hand. In her body.

She had trusted him that much.

Looking at him now, though, she was afraid of him. Because that fierce, burning passion he'd shown before was still there. And once again, it was directed at her. But this time, it had taken a deadly turn.

CHAPTER TWO

CASSIE'S glance wavered. Strayed from his face to the closed door across the room; to the telephone mere inches away. If she moved quickly, she could scoot past him and be in the safety of the outer office before he realized her intent. If she leaned forward a fraction, she could punch the speaker button on the phone console, and call for help.

Either was preferable to her current predicament. Neither, though, proved to be an option.

"No, Cassandra," he said, interpreting her thoughts all too accurately. "You will neither leave this room, nor call for reinforcements—unless, of course, you'd prefer we discuss our situation in front of an audience?" He bent over her desk and lifted the telephone receiver. Dangled it in front of her nose. "If that's the case, then by all means go ahead. Alert every occupant in the building, if it pleases you. Or shall I do it for you?"

"Put that thing down!" she implored, furious at how feeble she sounded. Furious that, even when she felt threatened by him, she still found him fascinating—the moth drawn to a devastating flame.

"Certainly, *cara*. The last thing in the world I intend is to distress you anymore than I already have." Gently, he returned the phone to its cradle, then dropped into one of the chairs on the other side of the desk, stretched out his long legs, and said conversationally, "So, there is a baby on the way. How do you propose we deal with this unexpected turn of events?"

19

Somewhat reassured by his more reasonable tone, she said, "*We* don't. This isn't your problem, Benedict."

"A child is never a problem. But if I am the father, then it most assuredly becomes my concern." His dark brown gaze scrutinized her features, searching for indecision, for deceit. "*Is* this baby mine, Cassandra?"

If she'd thought she could get away with it, she'd have lied and said "no." But he'd already heard her admit the truth to Trish, and even if he hadn't, it was a simple enough matter these days to obtain irrefutable clinical proof of paternity. "It's yours."

"Then our next move is clear enough. We shall be married."

"*Married?*" she choked, laughter bubbling hysterically in her throat. "You must be joking!"

"About taking a wife? Hardly!"

"Then you're insane. Marriage between us…it's simply not possible."

"Do you have a husband you neglected to mention before now?"

"Of course I don't!"

"There you are then." He lifted his hand. "Since I have no wife, marriage between us is entirely possible."

"For heaven's sake, Benedict, we were together once, and that was nearly three months ago. Since then, I've heard not a word from you."

"I've been out of the country."

"Well, I haven't! I've been here every day. The telephone works around the world, and so does e-mail. But you elected not to use either one, which leads me to believe that, as far I was concerned, 'out of sight' meant 'out of mind' to you. That being the case, you'll understand, I'm sure, why I find the idea of your wanting to marry me completely ludicrous."

He examined his short, immaculate fingernails, seemed to find them satisfactory, and favored her with another glance. "It isn't a question of wanting. I consider it to be my obligation."

It wasn't *what* he said, so much as the calm resignation with which he said it, that started her crying again. Not outwardly—pride wouldn't allow that—but inside, it was as if he'd stabbed a sharp needle into her heart. She'd known clients negotiate business contracts with more warmth and emotion!

"I don't want a husband who sees me as an obligation," she said, when she trusted herself to speak again.

"What do you want in a husband, Cassandra?"

"Love, friendship, commitment, passion—none of which I'm likely to find with you."

"None?" he echoed lazily. "Do you not remember how it was for us, last New Year's Eve?"

Not remember? She'd have laughed at such a preposterous question if she hadn't suddenly found herself floundering in a wash of déjà vu so intense that her face burned. Whatever other elements might have been missing that night, passion hadn't been among them. "Yes. And as I said a moment ago, it was one time only."

"Yet even today, the mention of it stirs you. I think I can promise you more of the same. I'm a normal, red-blooded man—as you so succinctly pointed out to your friend, Patricia. And you, *cara,* although technically no longer a virgin, remain in many ways such an innocent that you can't begin to know the power of sex—of how it can tame even the most reluctant heart, or weld the most unlikely union." From the table beside him, he picked up the art deco figure of a woman, and traced his finger over her eyelids and down her cheek to her throat. "It will be my very great privilege to instruct you."

He might as well have touched Cassie. Her flush deepened, spread. Raced the length of her body until it found its mark, and bathed her panties in dew.

Sometimes, the obstetrician had informed her, as he detailed what she could expect over the next six and a half months if everything went according to plan, *women lose all interest in sex during their pregnancies. Others can't seem to get enough of it.*

Was she, she wondered mournfully, destined to belong to the latter group? Was there no end to the day's humiliation? Hadn't she enough to contend with already?

Embarrassed, she squirmed in the chair, despising the tiny electric charge pulsing between her legs. And Benedict...he *smiled.* He *knew!*

"I don't want to have this discussion with you, especially not now, and definitely not here," she said.

"I can see that." Replacing the statuette, he eased himself out of the chair. "We'll continue it this evening then. I can arrange for a private dinner in my hotel suite, if you like, or shall I come to your home?"

Neither, if she had a choice. But the hard, determined set of his jaw told her that if she refused to see him, he'd simply waylay her the next time she set foot in the office. And he might not be quite so discreet, the next time!

She grabbed a pen. Scribbled on a notepad, tore off the page, and thrust it at him. "To my home," she said from between clenched teeth. "Here's the address."

At least she'd be in control there. Could show him the door when she'd had enough.

"At what time?"

"Seven o'clock. But don't expect anything elaborate

in the way of food. Mealtimes are a bit of a trial for me, at the moment.''

"I understand.'' He nodded, and assuming that was his way of taking his leave, she thought he'd make straight for the door. Instead, he came around the desk toward her.

As hastily as her queasy stomach would allow, she sprang up from the chair. She felt at enough of a disadvantage as it was, without having him loom over her even more than his eight-inch height advantage already allowed.

"Goodbye,'' she said, and thrust out her right hand. It might be a ridiculous gesture, considering she was carrying his baby and he'd just proposed, but it was safer to keep things formal.

Unfortunately, he had other ideas, though she didn't at first realize it. Instead of shaking her hand, as she'd intended he should, he turned it over and, dipping his head, kissed the inside of her wrist, right on the pulse point.

Her blood leaped wildly, and she let out a muffled squeak of surprise, at which he smoothed open her tightly clenched fingers and planted another, slower kiss on the palm of her hand. Then he lifted his head a fraction, blinked so that his lashes brushed over the skin of her arm, murmured, *"Arrivederci,* Cassandra,'' and a moment later, the door clicked shut behind him.

With sunset, the air turned cool enough to warrant putting a match to the kindling in the hearth. Once the flames took hold, Cassie threw on two small logs, then stood back and spared one last glance around the living room.

The silk-shaded lamp on the desk cast gentle shadows

over the curved ceiling, and painted an overlay of gold on the glass doors of the built-in bookcases on each side of the river rock fireplace. An arrangement of fresh arum lilies stood in the bay window, the blooms creamy white against the navy background of sky outside.

A small epergne of pink roses, tall candles, and her grandmother's china graced the table in the dining alcove. In the kitchen, Veal Prince Orloff simmered in the oven. A bottle of white burgundy chilled in the refrigerator.

Had she gone to too much trouble? Made it look as if she cared what Benedict Constantino thought of her style and taste? Should she have made the occasion more casual, and served pizza in the den, with the TV turned to the evening news, instead of playing Claude Debussy's Piano Preludes playing softly on the stereo? Should she have chosen to wear jeans and a sweater, rather than a long silk caftan and pearls?

Uncertain, excited, nervous, she was on the point of returning to the bedroom to change, when the downstairs buzzer sounded. Peering from the living-room window, she saw Benedict standing under the awning on the street below, perusing the list of other residents in the building. He had on what appeared to be the same dark suit he'd worn earlier. Probably the same shirt and tie, too. He might be willing to marry her, but clearly didn't give a rap about impressing her!

"Something smells wonderful," he said, when he arrived at her door on the second floor. Then, to put paid to any notion she might entertain that he was referring to her perfume, added, "I thought Patricia was the expert chef in your partnership."

"She is. I shopped at a gourmet deli on the way home. The only thing I've contributed to the meal is the salad."

It wasn't the same suit, after all, but another superbly tailored effort in dark gray, with a shirt the color of mist, and a silk tie midway between the two shades. He looked altogether too divine for her to handle with equanimity, and to stop herself from staring, she buried her nose in the flowers he'd brought. "Mmm, freesias! How did you know they're one of my favorites?"

"Why else would you have them growing outside your office window?"

"You noticed? Well, thank you. They're lovely."

"Prego!" He smiled—something else she found disturbingly attractive.

Indicating the living room, she said, "Make yourself comfortable while I find a vase for them."

"I would have brought wine," he remarked, ignoring her direction and following her into the kitchen, "but I assume you're avoiding alcohol these days."

"You assume correctly. But that doesn't mean you can't enjoy a predinner drink. You have the choice of scotch, sherry, campari or wine."

"Perhaps a glass of wine later, with the meal. For now, I'm content to watch you."

Another of those annoying flushes stole up her neck. "I wish you wouldn't say things like that."

"Why not? I enjoy looking at you, which is a good thing, since you're about to become my wife and we'll be seeing rather a lot of each other."

"That hasn't been decided, Benedict," she said firmly. "I've yet to be convinced there's any merit to your proposal."

"But certainly there is," he said, his Italian accent suddenly more pronounced. "In my country, a man marries the mother of his child. It's as simple as that."

"But this is the United States. Things are done differently here."

"Differently, perhaps, but that doesn't make them better, or right." He touched her cheek. "You're troubled that we're not in love, but where I was born, it used to be that other factors carried more weight when it came to marriage, such as building respect for one's spouse, and working together to create a good home for one's children. If love of the kind you're referring to entered the picture, it was by coincidence and deemed a secondary consideration."

"In other words, you're talking about arranged marriages." She tossed her head contemptuously. "Maybe there are some women who don't mind being treated like chattels, but I'm not one of them."

"Arranged, yes, but also lasting. Divorce was unheard of in my parents' day, Cassandra. Family came first, and all the rest—the fondness between a man and his wife, the devotion—fell into place after that. Even now, seldom does a widow of my mother's generation choose to remarry—surely a powerful endorsement of the durability of a union based on reason rather than romance?"

"That's one way of looking at it, I suppose. But it could just as well be that, having at last gotten out from under one man's thumb, she's in no hurry to repeat the experience with another."

He laughed, a low husky sound that sent his breath rippling warmly against her neck. "Are you afraid I'll hold *you* under my thumb, *cara?*"

"Not in the least."

"That's good. Because I can think of many more pleasurable ways to keep my bride close."

"Well, I hope she enjoys them, whoever she is." Cassie picked up the vase and carried it through to the living room, leaving him to accompany her or not, as he pleased. "But you might as well accept that it won't be me, Benedict. I have no intention of settling for a marriage based on *fondness*."

He followed her down the hall, his footsteps slow and measured on the planked oak floor. "You *will* marry me," he said, with unshakable confidence. "The only thing yet to be decided is how long it will take for me to convince you of it."

She looked past where he'd stationed himself near the fire, to the carriage clock on the mantel behind him. "Think in terms of two hours, Benedict. I plan to be in bed, *alone*, no later than half past nine."

"You're not feeling well?"

"Apart from a little queasiness now and then, I'm perfectly fine," she lied, unwilling to give him another reason to pressure her. "My doctor said everything's proceeding swimmingly."

Actually, what he'd said was, *I don't want to alarm you unnecessarily, but your cervix is a little softer than it should be in a woman at this stage of her first pregnancy, so I'm sending you for a sonogram sooner than usual. If the results warrant it, we need to take preventative measures to minimize the risk of a premature birth, or miscarriage.*

When she'd first suspected she might be pregnant, she'd been ambivalent about the idea. But the specter of possible miscarriage terrified her. Only then had she realized how much, during those early weeks, she'd connected with the tiny life growing inside her.

What sort of measures? she'd asked.

The medical term for the procedure is a Circlage. It involves a local anesthetic and the placing of sutures through and around the cervix, thereby drawing the opening firmly closed. In layman's language, it's sometimes referred to as "the purse string" operation, which actually describes it rather well. The sutures are removed around the thirty-sixth week of pregnancy, to allow for normal dilation of the cervix as birth becomes imminent.

Is there any risk to the baby?

Some slight risk, yes, but the earlier the procedure is performed, the safer it is for both mother and child, which is why I'm bringing it to your attention now.

"If everything's going swimmingly," Benedict said, interrupting her thoughts so suddenly that she almost dropped the vase, "why are you looking so apprehensive? What aren't you telling me, Cassandra?"

"Nothing. I'm wondering if I'm overcooking the Veal Prince Orloff, that's all."

"I can't imagine that gazing pensively at a container of freesias is going to give you the answer."

"You're right," she said, placing the flower arrangement on the corner table between the sofas. "Excuse me while I check the oven."

This time, he didn't follow her and when she returned to the living room, she found him examining the framed antique floral prints on the wall. "You have some very fine things in your home, *cara*."

"Much of what you see I inherited."

He strolled about the room, stopping to admire the voluptuous shape and contrasting wood of her prized bombé chest, and ended up in the arched entrance to the dining alcove. "And the rest?"

"I bought. Haunting antique auctions is one of my hobbies."

"You have excellent taste."

"Thank you." The reception rooms were large, but he made them seem cramped and airless. If he wasn't standing close enough to ruffle her hair with his breath, his shadow was reaching out to touch her.

She found it unsettling. The sooner he was gone, the better. "We should start on our first course. The veal is almost done."

He pulled out her chair at the head of the long, oval table, took his own place opposite and, while she served the asparagus soup, poured himself a glass of the wine chilling in a silver wine cooler at his elbow.

"I very much appreciate this," he commented, breaking apart a fluffy dinner roll still hot from the oven. "Hotel food serves well enough when it must, but it doesn't approach the pleasure found in a home-prepared meal."

She could hardly take exception to that and for the next fifteen minutes or so, they exchanged the kind of pleasant small talk any couple might enjoy. Relaxing despite her previous reservations, Cassie was able to manage her soup and a small helping of the salad which followed.

It was a different story with the main course. The rich combination of veal layered with mushrooms and onion, and covered with cheese sauce, was more than she could stomach. And of course, Benedict noticed.

"You're not eating, Cassandra," he remarked, eyeing the way she was pushing the food around her plate with very little of it making its way to her mouth.

"I'm suddenly not very hungry."

"Isn't it a bit late in the day for morning sickness?"

"My body doesn't seem able to tell the time."

"You've discussed this with a doctor?"

"Yes."

"And?"

"And nothing." She sipped her ice water and prayed she wouldn't have to make an undignified dash for the bathroom. "My digestive problems don't exactly make for sparkling dinner conversation. Can we please talk about something else?"

"If you wish. But I'd like the name of this doctor."

"Why?" Her stomach rumbled a warning.

"To satisfy myself that he's competent."

"He's more than just a run-of-the-mill doctor. He's an obstetrician. He specializes in pregnancies."

"So you say."

"Don't you believe me?"

He regarded her silently a moment, then said, "Yes, but I'm not sure I believe you've told me everything there is to know. I'm anxious about you."

This time, it was more than a warning. This time, her stomach heaved a protest. "Well, don't be. I'm in very good hands."

"I intend to make sure that you are. I intend to speak with this doctor, with or without your cooperation."

She took another cautious sip of ice water and, as calmly as she could, said, "No. It's none of your concern."

"It's very much my concern, Cassandra. Make no mistake about that."

"Perhaps you haven't heard about doctor-patient confidentiality. You don't have the *right* to information about me."

"*Not have the right?* As the father of your child, I have *every* right, and I assure you I intend to exercise it."

The edge in his voice unnerved her. Rumor had it that he was wealthy, a tycoon with international connections;

that he represented his family's North American business interests, and acted as its transaction agent and import specialist. He was undoubtedly accustomed to negotiating with other powerful magnates and coming out on top.

And she? At her best, she'd be hard-pressed to beat him at his own game. In her present condition, she was in no shape to go toe-to-toe with him on the weather, let alone his paternal rights.

Right on cue, Prince Orloff's veal swirled unpleasantly in her stomach. She clamped her napkin to her mouth and pushed away from the table.

"Excuse me," she muttered, and fled.

When she came back some fifteen minutes later to discover the dining room dark and only the lamp on the desk burning, she thought he'd left. Dispirited at finding her relief mixed with regret—did she want his attention, or not?—she sank onto the couch and folded her legs under her. But no sooner was she settled than footsteps approaching from the kitchen told her he hadn't abandoned her, after all.

A second later he came into the living room.

"I brought you some tea and dry toast," he said, placing a tray on the coffee table, and the genuine concern in his voice brought tears trembling to her lashes. "Sorry it took me so long. I had to find my way around your kitchen. Hope you don't mind."

"No," she said. "How did you know to do this— serve me dry toast, that is?"

"I have two nephews, and well remember the misery they caused my sister before they were born. This was her remedy and she swore by it."

Cassie sipped from the cup he passed to her, aware

that he watched the entire time, that he missed not a flicker of expression on her face.

Eventually he said, "What is it, *cara?* Do I make such dreadful tea, that you look so unhappy?"

Again, the compassion in his voice undid her. Helplessly, she shook her head and pressed her lips together, struggling to hang on to her composure. Even when she felt able to speak again, her voice remained thick with tears. "The tea's fine. It's everything else...."

"I'm sorry about the baby. Not that I wish it harm, but that it was conceived so carelessly." He took her hand and covered it with both of his. "I blame myself, Cassandra. I'm past the age where such impulses are forgivable in a man which is why I beg you to let me atone in the best way I know how."

His hand slid up her arm, caressed her shoulder, slipped inside the loose cowl collar of her caftan and cupped the back of her neck.

She flinched at his touch—so gentle, so subtly erotic. How was she supposed to remain immune to it? To cling to her resolve not to weaken under his persuasion?

"Are you afraid of me?" he asked.

"Yes," she said, looking him straight in the eye.

"Will you tell me why?"

She fell silent then because she daren't admit how insidious her attraction to him was.

He continued to watch her, to stroke her nape. After a while, he said, "What happened, that you grew up without a father, Cassandra?"

"I was conceived before my parents married. My father stayed around long enough to know he had a daughter, then left my mother and me for another woman when I was seventeen months old. We never heard from him again."

"That won't happen to us. I give you my word that I'll honor my wedding vows. I will take care of you and our child."

"I don't need taking care of," she told him, even though a part of her yearned to accept what he offered. Just once, it would be nice to know how it felt to have a strong male shoulder to lean on, a big warm masculine body to curl up against at night. "If my mother could take care of herself and a child, I can."

"Don't you see that you shouldn't have to? That this is a shared responsibility?"

"I'm not saying I won't let you be part of this baby's life. That wouldn't be fair to either of you."

"That's not what you told Patricia this morning. I distinctly heard you say it hadn't hurt you growing up without a father. You also said you weren't going to tell me you're pregnant."

"Well, I feel differently now, since you found out anyway and it turns out that, unlike my father, you don't mind being saddled with a child."

His long, strong fingers massaged the tension knotting the base of her neck. In the warm, drugging sense of relief that followed, it was all she could not to groan with pleasure. "Or with that child's mother," he whispered against her ear.

Like the first warning tremor of an approaching earthquake, she felt her resistance waver and begin to topple frighteningly close to acquiescence. Sidestepping the danger just in time, she pulled away from him and said, "Stop pressuring me, Benedict. I've had enough for one day."

"Then we'll leave it for now, and talk again when you're feeling more rested. Thank you for allowing me to come here, and for the wonderful dinner."

"Hardly wonderful! I never got around to offering you dessert or coffee," she said, on a small laugh.

He rose and shot his cuffs into place. "You offered a glimpse inside your head and your heart, *cara.* There isn't a dessert in the world to compare with that."

"How long will you be in town?" she asked, following him to the foyer and opening the front door.

He paused on the threshold and looked down at her. His remarkable eyes, so dark a brown they were almost black, caressed her face, feature by feature. His silky lashes drooped lazily at half-mast, as though concealing a joke he wasn't ready to share. "As long as it takes for you to learn to trust me," he said, and pressed his lips to her cheek.

They stayed there too long, took vaguely erotic liberties against her skin, and she opened her mouth to tell him so. He promptly took advantage of her error. So swiftly and smoothly she was caught completely off guard, his lips covered hers, and there was nothing the least bit vague about their message this time.

They spoke of raw passion barely held in check. Of wicked, delicious midnight-dark delight hers to enjoy if only she'd let herself. They stole the very things she most needed to cling to: her sense of purpose, her conviction—and a little bit more of her heart.

And the reprimand she'd been about to hurl at him? Poor thing, it simply withered in the heat of his kiss. Died without a murmur or even a whimper.

"As long as it takes, *mi amore,*" he said again, and leaving her clinging limply to the door frame, he ran swiftly down the stairs and out to the street.

She shut her door, rammed home the dead bolt, and tottered back to the living room where the snack he'd prepared remained virtually untouched. Suddenly starving, she devoured the toast, drank the tea and, appetite still not satisfied, swept up the tray and went to the kitchen.

She saw at once that he'd made himself useful while she was busy throwing up. The leftovers from dinner were stored in the refrigerator, the china and silver rinsed and loaded in the dishwasher.

It's difficult to nurture immunity toward a man as thoughtful as this, she decided, boiling water to make a poached egg, and popping another slice of bread in the toaster. *Maybe I'm being too rash in rejecting his proposal out of hand. Maybe New Year's Eve wasn't an end in itself, but the beginning of something incredible. Maybe, against all odds, I've found the man destiny created me for.*

If she could be sure he was right in saying that a marriage was stronger for being founded on trust, respect and family values, with a soupcon of chemistry thrown in for good measure, she might be willing to take the plunge. If, as well, there was some hope, however slender, that the potential for consuming love might also be in the cards, she'd definitely consider it worth the risk.

She broke an egg into a cup, swirled the boiling water vigorously, and dropped the egg in the eye of the vortex she'd created. While it cooked, she buttered the toast lightly, and poured herself a glass of milk.

He had been kind and thoughtful. He wanted to be a physical presence in his child's life. He'd shown concern for her physical well-being, her mental state. They weren't bad qualities in a father, a husband. She could do a lot worse.

How long will you be in town?

As long as it takes for you to learn to trust me…as long as it takes, mi amore….

How long was that?

The egg was done. She scooped it onto a slotted spoon, let it drain a moment, then slid it, all fluffy white around the edges with a hint of yellow at its center, onto the toast. Drizzled on a little salt, a speck of pepper. For the first time in days, the smell of the food—melting butter, hot, fresh egg—made her mouth water.

She stacked everything on the tray he'd used earlier, and carried it to the window nook overlooking the terrace. Her daytime planner lay face down in the middle of the little wrought-iron table where she normally ate breakfast. When she turned the book over, she found it open at that day's page. It showed her obstetrician's name and telephone number, as well as the time of her appointment that morning. And on the floor, where it must have fallen without his noticing, was a business card with Benedict Constantino's name on it.

She didn't have to be a mental giant to figure out what had taken place while she'd been losing her dinner.

I had to find my way around your kitchen. Hope you don't mind....

How about, *I snooped through your private possessions?* she thought furiously. How about, *I made a note of your doctor's name and phone number on one of my business cards and didn't notice that I'd pulled out two by mistake and left the second behind as evidence of my deception?*

All at once, the egg smelled like sulfur. Looked as slippery as he was. So much for his professed concern! He must have gloated all the way back to his hotel at how easily he'd hoodwinked her!

"How long before I learn to trust you, Benedict?" she muttered bitterly, shoveling the toast and egg into the sink and flushing it down the waste disposer. "When hell freezes over, that's when, and not a minute sooner!"

CHAPTER THREE

"WELL, at least he's got good taste." Trish brushed a gentle finger over the mist of baby's breath interspersed among the six dozen long-stemmed pink roses overshadowing everything else on the board-room table. "If you won't have them in your office, I'll take them in mine."

"Take them, and Benedict Constantino as well!" Cassie fumed.

"I don't think it's me he wants, dearie. I think he's prepared to do whatever it takes to make sure he winds up with you."

"Then all I can say is, he's got some strange ideas of how to go about it, if he thinks rifling through my personal records is the way to win me over."

"He looked at your daybook, for heaven's sake, not stole your inheritance out from under you! And from what you've told me, you pretty much drove him to it."

"I might have known you'd take his side. You've never been able to resist tall, black-haired men."

"I'm not taking anyone's side," Trish said, in the sort of reasonable tone an adult might adopt when dealing with a fractious child. "I'm trying to make you see reason. The man obviously cares about you. Since when is that a crime?"

"Since he resorted to conniving tactics, that's when! It shows an underhanded side to his character that I don't care for. And it goes beyond what he did last night, Trish. Don't forget he also eavesdropped on a conversation between you and me, and made not the slightest attempt to announce himself.''

''He probably didn't feel you left him any other choice. If it had been up to you, he'd still be in the dark about the pregnancy. How's he supposed to know what else you might be keeping from him?'' She cast a last envious glance at the arrangement of roses. ''And regardless of his sins, imagined or otherwise, there's no denying he's earned a few Brownie points with these. Even the container is gorgeous.''

''It's ostentatious.'' Cassie glared at the huge crystal bowl, easily the size of a medicine ball with the top cut off. ''Talk about overkill! Your problem is that you're a pushover for appearances.''

''Well, what else do you expect? I'm a chef. Quality and presentation are everything. And whether or not you admit it, that's one beautiful vase, Cassie.''

''Vase?'' Cassie sniffed disparagingly, and tried not to be swayed by the alluring scent of roses she managed to inhale along with a healthy dose of indignation. ''I could practically take a bath in it!''

''Not for much longer. Pretty soon, you won't fit through the opening.''

''You're not helping matters, Patricia!''

''Yes, I am,'' her friend said. ''I'm doing my level best to make you face the facts without blowing everything out of proportion. Benedict didn't have to offer to marry you. He didn't even have to take your word for it that he's the baby's father. That he did both without hesitation says a lot more about the kind of man he is, than the fact that he took an uninvited look at your day book or listened in on a conversation some people might argue he had a right to hear. He's a rare specimen in this day and age, and you'd be a fool not to at least consider his proposal.''

''But we're not in love!''

Expression somber, Trish looked away. ''Maybe not, but you were in lust enough to get pregnant by him, and that ought to take precedence over all else. It would, if I were in your place.''

''I know it would,'' Cassie said contritely. Trish and her husband Ian had been trying for a baby for over three years, without success. ''I'm sorry, Trish. You're the last person I should be confiding in about this.''

''That's what friends are all about—to lend an ear when it's needed, and dole out advice whether it's needed or not. Besides, who else can you trust but me to set you straight?''

Not a soul! She had no siblings, no aunts or uncles or cousins—at least, none that she knew about. Trish was more than just her dearest friend; she was like a sister and, since Cassie's mother's death the previous October, the closest thing to family Cassie had. She had other friends, of course, but none as loyal or trustworthy. None who knew her so well, nor any whose opinion she valued more.

''You really think I'm judging him too harshly?''

''I think you're being hasty. It would be different if you couldn't stand to be around him. But Cassie, you should see your face when you talk about him! You might wish you could hate him, but the simple fact of the matter is, you can't. You're *very* attracted to him. And it's pretty clear he's just as taken with you.''

''He's interested in our baby. I just happen to be the womb in which it's planted.''

''Oh, give me a break! If that's the case, what was he

doing here yesterday, before he even knew you were pregnant?''

Cassie shrugged. "I neither know nor care."

"Well, sooner or later, you're going to have to come to grips with it, because he's not going to conveniently disappear. He came back to see you for some unknown reason, and found another, more compelling reason to stick around. So far, he's made all the concessions, and these…" Trish touched the tip of her finger to one perfect pink rose and sighed. "These are a blatant message that he's willing to make a few more."

"They're just flowers, for heaven's sake! A 'thank you for the dinner' gesture."

"No. If that's all he was trying to say, a potted plant would have done the job."

"So what are you suggesting—that I just cave in to his demands because he bought out a florist's entire supply of roses?"

"I'm suggesting that you make the next move and show yourself to be amenable to discussion and compromise." Trish picked up the phone. "And I'm suggesting you do it now. Because although he might be tall in stature, I suspect our gorgeous Italian is pretty short on tolerance when it comes to being pushed around. If you insist on playing hardball with Benedict Constantino, you'll be taking on a lot more than you can handle."

She was going to throw up again! And the manner in which Trish was waving the phone around in such a way that it looked like a cobra about to strike didn't help any! "I don't know where he's staying."

"You know his cell phone number. It's printed right there on his card."

"But he won't appreciate being disturbed during business hours. I'm not the primary reason he's in town. He's here to work, or visit his good friend Nuncio.''

"He'll have voice mail." The coiled phone cord writhed, the handset bobbed menacingly. "You can leave a message."

"Saying what?"

"Oh, I don't know. Something complicated and obtuse, such as 'Hello, Benedict, this is Cassandra. Please give me a call when you have a moment free.'

"If I do that, will you then leave me to wallow in my own misery?"

"Absolutely." Trish thrust the phone at her.

Wearily, Cassie punched in his number and prepared to deliver her message to some impersonal answering service.

He picked up on the first ring. Thoroughly unhinged, as much by the deep, sexy timbre of his voice as the fact that she was left suddenly tongue-tied, Cassie held the phone away and stared at it in horror. She'd have hung up on him, if Trish hadn't muttered in a stage whisper people in the next room probably heard, "Say something, Cass!"

"Cassandra?" Her name flowed from the ear piece like music, a melodic cascade of sound about two octaves below middle C.

"Hell...o...." she croaked.

"Ah," he said. Just that, followed by a pause as pregnant as she was.

Desperate to fill it, she babbled, "Thank you for the roses. They're lovely. Pink is my favorite. You shouldn't have. It wasn't necessary."

Trish snickered, covered her mouth with her hand, and turned away.

"It was entirely necessary, Cassandra," he said smoothly, dark, quiet laughter lacing his answer. "It was also my pleasure." When she didn't reply, he let the silence spin out a second or two more, then asked, "Is that the only reason you called?"

"Um…no."

Another, longer pause ensued, teeming with tension. At last, he said gently, "And the other?"

"I don't—can't…I don't like doing it on the phone."

Good grief, that sounded indecent! Obscene! And from the way Trisha turned purple, grabbed a tissue, and choked into it, she obviously thought so, too!

Drawing in a calming breath, Cassie started over. "What I'm trying to say is, I'd just as soon discuss the matter with you in person. Face-to-face."

"*Senz'altro*—of course! But this time, you won't cook for me. Instead, I'll take you to dinner at a favorite *ristorante* of mine, a quiet, tranquil—"

"No!" she said hastily, wishing his lilting accent didn't turn even the simplest remark into a caress. "Not dinner."

"Lunch, then."

"Yes."

"Today."

"Yes."

"*Eccellente!* I'll pick you up—"

"No," she said again, not about to find herself confined in a car with him, or hustled into some dark and intimate restaurant. "There's a sandwich shop in the lobby of my office building. I'll see you there at noon."

"If you insist," he said, sounding as if she'd suggested they meet at the city dump.

"I insist."

"You look somewhat discomposed," Trish tittered, when the call ended.

"More like *de*composed!" Cassie grabbed a binder and used it as a fan to cool her face. "I don't know what it is about that man that sets me off like this."

"Beyond finding him fatally attractive, you mean?"

"Is that really what it is? I'm drawn to dangerous men?"

"He's hardly dangerous, Cass!"

"Yes, he is," Cassie said. "There's something…iron hard underneath that charmingly compliant front he puts on."

"That shouldn't come as any surprise. How else do you suppose he climbed to the top of the tycoon heap? In any case, you'd never have let yourself be seduced by a pantywaist." Trish's eyes glimmered with further amusement. "Or did you seduce him, you little devil?"

"I most certainly did not!"

"No invitational glances in the moonlight? No locked gazes across a crowded deck?"

Cassie opened her mouth to refute those suggestions, too, then snapped it shut again, swamped in sudden, guilty memories….

"Will you dance with me, *signorina?*"

"I shouldn't. I'm here to work."

But she'd gone into his arms anyway. Let him hold her close enough to be vibrantly conscious of the lean strength of his torso, his long, powerful legs. Across San Francisco Bay, a premature burst of fireworks littered the sky with sprays of silver and gold, and a little of their sparkle inexplicably landed on her and left her glowing from the inside out.

"I hadn't expected you'd be here alone," he said, smiling down at her.

"I hadn't expected to be here at all," she said, "but

our social convener came down with the flu, and finding someone able to take over her job at short notice, especially on the busiest night of the year, was impossible.''

He tightened his hold, gave her hand a meaningful squeeze. ''How unfortunate that your employee fell ill—and what a stroke of good luck for me.''

Aware of his jaw grazing the crown of her head, of his fingers warmly enfolding hers, and most of all, of the current of untoward excitement coursing through her blood, she said, ''I'm very glad that you're enjoying your evening, Mr. Constantino, but you'll have to excuse me now. I really must get back to work and make sure Mr. Zanetti's guests have everything they need.''

''You're already working,'' he replied. ''You're making sure I have everything *I* need.''

A simmering heat had begun to consume her, and with every word, every nuance of meaning, he stoked the flames a little higher. Breathless, she'd tried to extricate herself from a situation she felt powerless to control.

As if he sensed she was on the brink of flight, he pulled her closer, not enough that anyone else would have noticed and made comment, but close enough for her to understand the specific nature of his ''need.''

But did she rebuff him? Stalk off in a snit? Fell him with a haughty glare?

Not a bit! She melted against him and when the music stopped, she withdrew from his hold with marked reluctance, an inch at a time, until only the tips of her fingers touched his. Apart from the fire in his dark eyes, he looked entirely collected. Of all the people on the covered, candlelit afterdeck, only she knew how provocatively other, more distant parts of his body had stirred against her. But *she* was burning all over, from her cheeks to her knees, and half expected to find the silk of her ivory cocktail dress singed everywhere he'd touched it.

"Thank you for the dance," she stammered, desperately trying to project a semblance of poise, and failing miserably.

But he, with his signature elegance of manner, murmured, "*Grazie,* Cassandra? *Per favore,* the honor was mine! That it's been so short-lived is my only regret."

Afraid that if she didn't turn away, she'd fly back into his arms, she'd sped—as much as her high heels would allow—back to her station in the main saloon where Trish's senior assistant was supervising the final preparations for the buffet supper. For the next hour, she lent a hand where one was needed, but although her fingers were kept otherwise engaged, her thoughts continued to dwell on Benedict Constantino.

Given his parting remark, perhaps she ought to have been suspicious when, half an hour before midnight, a crew member came to inform her she was urgently needed below deck. But fearing someone had been taken ill, she put Benedict out of her mind and followed the crewman down to the private quarters located in the stern of the boat.

The entrance to the suite had been unlocked, and although the lamp gleaming softly on the polished mahogany walls of the little foyer no sign of anyone waiting there, a swath of light fell dimly from the sitting room where she sometimes worked. Well, that made sense, she supposed.

She turned to tell the crewman that she'd take matters from there and he could return to his duties on the bridge, only to find he'd already left and closed the door behind him. More puzzled by the second, she crossed to the sitting room, peeped inside, and gasped audibly.

A dozen or more candles flickered about the cabin. On a table covered with a snowy linen cloth stood a silver wine cooler containing a bottle of champagne. Two crystal glasses, clouded with frost, and a single red rose in a bud vase completed the setting. And lounging against the bulkhead beside the window, with his jacket unbuttoned and his hands in his pockets, was Benedict Constantino.

Caught between vexation and amusement, Cassie said, "I hope you have a good explanation for this. I was led to believe there was some sort of emergency down here."

"But indeed there is, Cassandra," he replied, unfazed. "I most urgently need to be alone with you."

Repressing the little melting burst of delight brought on by his words, she said, "Very flattering, I'm sure, *Signor* Constantino, but it's hardly appropriate for me to single out one guest and neglect the rest."

He came to her and caught her hands in his. "Listen!" he commanded, drawing her to him and indicating with a nod of his handsome head the sounds of revelry taking place on the deck above them. "Does that sound to you like a crowd of people suffering from neglect?"

"That's hardly the point," she protested faintly.

"Indeed not," he murmured against her mouth. "But this most certainly is."

And he kissed her. Very thoroughly.

And she…she couldn't help herself. She kissed him back. The instant his lips touched hers, she was consumed with hunger. His to do with as he wished.

Fortunately, he wasn't quite as lacking in self-control. "That," he said hoarsely, putting her from him with hands which shook a little, "was premature, and by no means my primary reason for luring you down here."

"Oh," she whimpered, past caring that she sounded woefully disappointed. "What *was* the reason, then?"

"To welcome the new year in seclusion, with you."

"But that's not possible! They'll be expecting me on deck."

"Not for another twenty minutes, *cara,*" he said, leaving her weak-kneed with all sorts of vague and prohibited longing, while he attended to the business of uncorking the wine. "Admittedly not an ideal length of time, but certainly long enough for us to toast one another in private."

The champagne foamed exuberantly in the glasses, in much the same way that her blood sang through her veins as he offered her one of the flutes.

"I really shouldn't," she protested weakly, knowing perfectly well that she really would.

"It's but a little sin," he said, his voice wrapping her in velvet. "Nothing at all to lose sleep over." He raised his own glass, clinked it lightly against hers. "*Buona fortuna,* Cassandra! May the coming year see the fulfillment of all your dreams."

"Thank you." She couldn't look at him. *Dare* not. She was too afraid of what he might see in her eyes, and even more terrified of what she might detect in his. "Is this how you always celebrate New Year's Eve?"

"Not quite," he said. "I make it a rule to avoid parties such as the one taking place on deck. I don't care to be obliged to kiss every woman present, simply as a matter of custom. In this instance, however, a different set of rules apply. I am only too happy to kiss you."

And he did. Again. More thoroughly than ever, in a lovely, hot, damp, searching exploration of her mouth that left her yearning against him. That had her parting her lips and letting him taste the champagne she'd sipped.

Exactly when matters progressed beyond a kiss she couldn't have said, because she was incapable of rational thought, let alone speech. All she knew was that, for the first time in her life, a man was holding her as if she were the most precious creature on earth, and she never wanted him to let go.

She didn't care that she knew next to nothing about him. That was the brain's department and her brain most definitely was not in charge at that moment. Reason had no place in what was happening, nor had caution or propriety.

What mattered was that he inspired in her the kind of wild sexual longing and quivering expectation she'd read about but never really believed in. Her skin vibrated with awareness of him, the very pores seeming to reach out to absorb the texture of him. When he slid his hand down her throat and dipped a finger into the valley between her breasts, a reckless greed took hold of her, making itself heard in tiny, inarticulate moans buried somewhere deep in her throat.

With shocking audacity, she covered his hand with hers. Guided it to her breast. Pressed herself against his palm in brazen offering.

He responded in kind, pinning her against his hips in such a way that awareness jolted through her. He was hard as a rock. Hot as a fire. Strong and pulsing with contained passion.

He found the zipper holding closed her dress and lowered it far enough that the wide shawl neck of her dress slid away from her shoulders. She wore cream satin underneath, trimmed with French lace. It whispered audacious permission for him to push it aside. And then—at last, praise heaven!—he was cupping her bare breast, and lowering his head to tug gently at her nipple as if he were seeking to rob her of her soul.

She very nearly cried out loud. Desire skittered over her, puckering her skin and puddling between her thighs. She ached inside, a heavy, crescendo of sensation, part pain, and part ecstasy.

When his hand slipped over the curve of her bottom and began inching up her skirt, anticipation became craving; hunger turned to greed. She wanted him touching her bare skin; wanted him to find that throbbing, hidden place and answer its silent, tormented pleas.

She wanted to touch him. To feel the silken weight of him against her palm; to make him groan and shudder uncontrollably, just as he made her.

Perhaps she said as much. Perhaps, because of the fever consuming her, the words came tumbling out involuntarily, raw and shockingly frank. *I want to see your penis, stroke it…help me…give me permission…!*

Yes, she must have said exactly that because, in the next instant, *he* was the one holding *her* hand captive, right *there,* where the fine black wool of his dress pants stretched taut and expectant over the swell of his erection. She fumbled with his zipper, too eager, too clumsy, and so he helped her, showing himself to her without shame.

He was beautiful beyond anything she'd ever known. At once primitive and elegant. Strong and smooth and vital.

Awestruck, she gazed at him. Touched him tentatively and, encouraged by his smothered exclamation, closed both her hands around him and reveled in the convulsive jerk of his flesh. "Am I doing this right?" she whispered. "Do you like it?"

He rolled his eyes, growled something explosive in Italian, and the next instant, she was lying flat on her back on the carpet, with the full skirt of her dress spread around her like a collapsed parachute. When he discovered her sheer silk stockings left the top of her legs bare, he brushed his lips along her inner thigh, and murmured, *"Tua pelle...perfetta."*

"I'm not sure what that means," she quavered, teetering on the fine edge of a dazzling unknown, "but it sounds wonderful."

He lifted his head and let his gaze drift over her, warm and caressing as a lazy tropical breeze. "Your skin, Cassandra, it is perfect. *You* are perfect."

Then he touched her, in the exact spot where her body cried out for him with thick, heavy tears. Swept his finger and his tongue over her, and finally, when she was weeping all over, and begging him to end the torture, he entered her. Filled her completely.

For a few divine minutes, the outside world ceased to exist. He *was* her world; her universe. And when she shattered in his arms mere seconds before he relinquished control of his own body, she felt as if she were stardust free-falling from heaven.

Up on the afterdeck, cheers and whistles broke out. Ships' horns echoed across the Bay. Fireworks exploded, filling the sky with fountains of color. But she, still caught up in the euphoria of spent passion, did not at first recognize their significance. Then, as reality seeped back, she stared up at him, horrified. "We missed midnight!"

He shrugged. "I doubt anyone noticed."

They weren't the words she wanted to hear. Too dispassionate by far, they brought her back to earth with a bang. Squirming with embarrassment, she turned her face away and he, taking the hint, rolled off her and sprang lithely to his feet. By the time she'd done the same, albeit less vigorously, he'd restored his clothing to order and merely looked slightly disheveled.

She, however, was a complete mess. Her panties hung from one ankle, and maintaining her dignity while she put them back where they belonged proved an exercise in futility. She'd lost one shoe; it sprawled upside down under the table, looking every bit as wanton as she now felt. Her dress was as crumpled as if she'd slept in it—which, to phrase it delicately, was pretty much what she'd done. In retrospect, though, and as the afterglow faded, a much uglier term assigned itself to her behavior.

Benedict cleared his throat. "Cassandra," he began.

"Don't!" she said sharply, refusing to meet his glance. "Don't say another word. Just please go and spare us both the embarrassment of trying to behave as if what just happened amounted to anything other than animal lust."

"And leave you in complete disarray? That would not be gentlemanly of me."

"*Gentlemanly?*" If she hadn't been so utterly mortified, she'd have laughed at the notion that he understood the meaning of the word. "It's a bit late to be thinking along those lines, Mr. Constantino."

"And more than a little late for such formality, *cara.* My name, as you very well know, is Benedict."

"Fine. Go back on deck, Benedict, before your good friend Nuncio comes looking for you. I'm not exactly dressed for company."

Not bothering to wait for his response, she marched to the bathroom and locked herself in. When she came out again fifteen minutes later, the only reminders that he'd ever set foot in the suite were the champagne flutes and half-empty bottle of 1992 Bollinger *Vieilles Vignes Francaises*....

Trish's face was a study in curiosity. "You appear to be having difficulty processing my question, Cass," she remarked snidely, "so let me rephrase it. Did you lead Benedict on?"

"If I did," Cassie said uncomfortably, "it was unintentional. I certainly didn't expect we'd end up having sex, and to be fair, I don't think he did, either."

"Obviously not, or one of you would have had the foresight to use protection, and you wouldn't now be facing your present dilemma." Trish eyed her sympathetically. "Do you think you could learn to love him in time?"

"It's possible."

"So you're not against the idea?"

"No," Cassie said. "I'm just afraid of it."

"Why is that?"

"For a start, he's such a control freak—one of those drag-you-off-by-the-hair, Me Master, You Slave types!"

"Fifty-one per cent wonderful, forty-nine per cent impossible, in other words." Trish lifted one shoulder in a nonchalant shrug. "Well, nobody's perfect, Cass, and I can't see you ever submitting to being molded to the underside of any man's heel, so I'm not worried on that score."

"Well, I am, because I don't want to wind up falling in love with a man who might never love me back. I'm not putting myself or my baby through the misery my mother went through when my father decided he'd had enough of the family scene."

"It's not fair to label Benedict with your father's sins of omission. He deserves to be judged on his own merit."

"I know—which is why I agreed to meet him again and take another look at our options."

"Then don't let me keep you. It's almost noon, and you need to apply a bit more blusher and some lip gloss. Nausea might make some women look pale and interesting, but it doesn't become you at all."

CHAPTER FOUR

SHE did not look well. Unaware that he was watching her from the other side of the lobby, she stepped out of the elevator, and hovered near a smoked-glass wall mirror to check her appearance. Apparently dissatisfied with what she saw, she fluffed a hand through her short blond hair, pinched her cheeks to give them added color, and retied the crimson scarf at her throat.

As if any of that was enough to disguise the mauve shadows beneath her eyes, or the general pallor underlying the carefully applied cosmetics!

"Oh, there you are!" she said, on a nervous breath, when he intercepted her as she mingled with the stream of people headed for the sandwich shop she'd mentioned. "Have you been waiting long?"

"Long enough to see that you need a change of pace from what this place has to offer." He took her elbow and steered her through the building's massive main entrance, and out into the street. "We'll eat in the park. I'm told there's one not five minutes walk from here."

"They don't serve lunch in the park," she objected, dragging her feet.

"There's a delicatessen two doors away. We'll get them to fix us a picnic."

"I don't have time for that. Half an hour is all I can spare."

"Make the time, Cassandra," he said flatly. "Half an hour isn't enough."

She wrenched her elbow free and flung him a resentful

glare. "I don't have much taste for petty dictators, either."

"And I seldom find it necessary to issue orders, but when the need arises, when a woman doesn't show the good sense she was born with, as is the case now, then I'm more than equal to the task." He took her arm again, and marched her into deli. "So, here we are, *cara mia*. What do you feel like ordering—besides my head on a plate?"

"Nothing," she snapped, pinching her lips into a tight line and stubbornly refusing to look at the selection of prepared foods arranged in the glass-fronted display case. "I'm not hungry."

"Then I'll decide for both of us."

"Why am I not surprised to hear that, I wonder?"

"Someone has to make sure you take proper care of yourself," he pointed out, "and who has a more vested interest in your health than I?"

She sighed and rolled her eyes. "Just get a move on, will you? I don't have all day, and we have more important issues waiting to be resolved than whether you want pastrami on rye for lunch, or smoked beef in a bun."

Then, as if the mention of food was enough to turn her stomach, she grew paler than ever, and hurried outside to sit in the shade of an umbrella at one of the sidewalk tables.

Keeping an eye on her to make sure she didn't bolt, he bought slices of cold roasted chicken breast, Melba toast squares, a small wedge of mild cheese, some pale green grapes, and two bottles of mineral water. "We can eat out here, if you wish," he said, joining her at the table.

But she shook her head. "No. I'd rather sit in the

park." She swallowed, mopped her glistening upper lip with a dainty handkerchief, and gestured weakly at the open door of the deli. "The smell in there…anything like that…it's overpowering these days."

"I understand. Do you feel up to the walk, or shall I call for a taxi?"

"Oh let's walk, and the sooner, the better!" She pointed across the street to a pedestrian lane winding between two apartment complexes. "We can take that short cut. It'll get us there in no time."

He put his hand in the small of her back while they waited for a break in the traffic, and couldn't help noticing not only that she looked unwell, but that she felt much more fragile than she had just over two months ago. Not that she'd ever been a big woman, but there'd been a sweet roundness to her arms and legs before, a gentle flare to her hips, a softer curve to her cheek.

Now, she was all skin and bone; fragile to the point of brittle. Still beautiful, of course—she had the kind of skeletal structure which would make her beautiful even when she was old and gray. But there was no bloom to her; no evidence of the radiance he'd witnessed in his sister when she'd been pregnant. Simply put, Cassandra looked ill.

"Still queasy?" he asked, as they left the buildings behind and followed a path over a grassy slope in the park to a sunlit glade where a little waterfall splashed into a pond.

"No," she said irritably. "Stop fussing! And stop looking at me as if you're afraid I'm going to drop dead at your feet."

But he wasn't deceived by her flimsy bravado. She was wilting visibly, and he regretted that he'd not gone along with her wish to remain in her office building.

Alas, where she was concerned, he regretted many things!

"Sit," he said, spreading his jacket on the grass.

This time, she didn't object to being told what to do. With obvious relief, she sank down with her legs tucked beneath her, and accepted the bottle of water he handed to her from the picnic box. "Thank you. You're very kind."

"I'm very concerned, Cassandra. You are too pale, too thin. What does your doctor have to say about this?"

"You mean to say, you didn't show up at his office first thing this morning, to ask him yourself?"

"How could I? You refused to tell me his name."

Two spots of angry color stained her cheeks, emphasizing the pallor of the rest of her face. "I'm in no mood for your lies, Benedict."

"What lies?" he asked, suppressing the surge of anger her accusation inspired. Had she been a man...! "I do not lie."

"How can you stand there looking so offended, when we both know you made it your business to find out who my doctor is, and we both know how you went about it?"

"I haven't the faintest idea what you're talking about," he told her stiffly. "Nor do I care for your tone."

"Oh, please!" She cast him an evil glance from under her lashes. "Drop the act! You're too sophisticated and about twenty years too late to carry off the role of injured innocent."

"I'm thirty-four, Cassandra, and yes, I'm a man of the world. But I've yet to master the art of mind reading. So, I repeat, I don't know what it is that you think I've done. Enlighten me, please, before I lose all patience."

"You made yourself at home in my kitchen last night."

"Indeed yes. And I explained why. I was trying to spare you having to clean up after the meal. Did I not meet your standards of housekeeping excellence?"

"Indeed, yes!" she exclaimed with heavy sarcasm. "You'll make some woman a fine wife, one day—either that, or an international spy!"

He'd never thought he'd find himself so livid with her when she looked so frail, but her last insult was something he would not overlook. "Are you so mired in middle-class mores that my turning my hand to domestic chores when you're ill makes me less of a man in your eyes? Because if so, Cassandra, then we have both made a grave error in judgment, I for believing you to be a woman of intelligence, and you for having taken me to be a fool."

To her credit, she had the grace to look ashamed. "I'm sorry. I shouldn't have said that about being someone's wife. But I'm sticking with your making a good spy."

"And why is that?"

"You found my day-planner."

"Yes," he said. "And the crime attached to having done so?"

"You looked in it. You deliberately sought out information which was none of your business."

"Take care," he warned her, and knew from the sudden wary look in her eyes that she felt the chill in his tone. "Because you're carrying my child, I'm willing to make allowances, but even you step on dangerous ground when you question my integrity and continue to fling unfounded accusations in my face. Don't push me too far, *mia bella gestante.* You might not like the out-come.''

Her eyes, a deep, enchanting blue, turned dark with suspicion. "What's a *gestante?*"

"An expectant mother. What did you think?"

"That if I'm tossing insults at you, you might be in-clined to toss a few back at me."

"No, Cassandra. I have other ways of getting even."

"I'm sure you have," she said, "but we're straying from the subject. If you weren't snooping for informa-tion last night, what was one of your business cards do-ing on the floor next to the table where I'd left my day-planner?"

"I planned to leave without saying goodbye. You were so long in your room, I thought perhaps you'd gone to bed because the sickness did not pass. So I took out one of my cards, to write a note telling you I'd be in touch later today, but found I'd left my pen in the brief-case in my car. I saw there was a pencil on the table and was about to use it when I heard you return to the *salone.* I forgot about the note then, and made you toast and tea instead. The card must have fallen to the floor without my noticing, perhaps because I thought it more important to attend to you in person. What was so ter-rible about that?"

She plucked at the blades of grass edging his jacket, and looked so abject that his irritation melted into com-passion. "Nothing," she said finally. "Except that I've made an idiot of myself over nothing. I seem to be doing that rather often, these days."

"It's a trying time for you," he said, wishing she didn't stir him so deeply. She was confident and suc-cessful, a woman of many talents and a great deal of charm. She didn't need his protection. And yet, he felt the need to look after her. Or was it the baby she carried that moved him so profoundly?

He couldn't say. Mother and child were inextricably bound together. They always would be.

Briefly, she met his gaze. "For you, too. A week ago, I'm sure you had no intention of asking me to marry you."

"That is true," he said. "A week ago, many things occupied my mind, but taking a wife was not among them."

"You see? That's why marriage is all wrong for us. We were never lovers in the real sense of the word, nor even friends. We're merely acquaintances."

"We are also adults, and therefore accountable for our actions. Our child is not to blame for having been conceived. This is a situation entirely of our own creating, and we have to make the best of it."

"You make it sound as simple as one and one adding up to two. But it's not."

He smiled. "Indeed no. In this case, one and one adds up to three—unless you happen to be carrying twins."

"Perish the thought! This is no joke, Benedict!"

"It doesn't have to be a tragedy, either." Drawing her to her feet, he grazed her chin with his knuckles, a fleeting caress only, and tried not to notice how, set in mutinous lines though it might be, her mouth remained temptingly delicious. It was obsessing about just such trifles that had landed him in so much trouble with her to begin with. "Look at me, Cassandra. Am I so hideous that you can't bring yourself to like me just a little? Do I repel you? Does the thought of my kissing you, touching you, leave you sick to your stomach?"

He saw the conflict in her eyes, the faint blush staining her cheeks, the erratic leap of her pulse at the corner of her jaw. "No," she admitted reluctantly. "If it did, I'd never have made love with you."

"Then let us build on that. The spark exists, *cara*. With luck and perseverance, we can fan it into a flame."

"But it's not that easy! It takes a lot more than one night of sex to build the solid foundation for marriage."

"You underestimate my determination," he told her. "When I set my sights on a goal, nothing stops me until I achieve it."

"Which I might find flattering if your goal was to win me. But we both know it isn't. If I weren't pregnant, you'd never have proposed."

"Are you so sure of that?"

"Well, *yes!* Let's not pretend otherwise."

"Very well, we won't pretend. Instead, we'll be brutally honest with one another. So here is the way I see things." He caught her hands in his. "I find you interesting and beautiful, both in mind and body. I admire your spirit and drive, the confidence and grace with which you approach life. We are sexually compatible. All good things for two people considering a lifelong union, yes?"

"I suppose so, but—"

He squeezed her fingers, drew her a fraction closer. "There is more. I believe in the sanctity of marriage, and of the family, and hold both sacred. I will allow nothing to harm either one. Although becoming a husband and father has happened sooner than I anticipated, I hold an aversion for neither. I shall honor you as my wife, and be proud to acknowledge you as the mother of my child. You will never want for material comfort or emotional support." He took a step backward, searched her face to learn something of what she was thinking, of what she might be feeling. "There, I am done. Now it's your turn."

"Oh," she said, a trifle breathlessly. "After all that, I hardly know what to say."

"You could tell me you don't believe me."

"But I do," she said ruefully. "That's half the trouble."

"It's half the battle, Cassandra. If you trust me enough to take my word on matters as important as these, how can marriage fail to bind us ever closer to one another?"

"You sound so sure."

"Because I am convinced this is the case."

"But there's so much we don't know about one another."

"We have the rest of our lives to learn, which is as it should be. A good marriage isn't static, *cara*. It continues to grow and become richer."

"I have to agree with you on that, but what about the logistics? My business is here on the West Coast, and you're based in New York."

"Only because it is closer to Europe and slightly more convenient. But with a wife and baby to think of, my priorities change and the world, after all, is a very small place. East Coast, West Coast, it makes little difference to me."

"You'd move here, just to be with me?"

"Yes, because it is important to you. And I hope, if the situation were reversed, that I could say the same of you. Otherwise, what use would we be to one another or our child?"

"Oh, Benedict," she sighed, leaning against him. "You make it very hard for me to turn you down."

"Then we'll be married? Is that what you're telling me?"

A trembling shudder ran over her, reminding him of a butterfly trapped in a net. "Oh, why not?" she whispered on an exhausted breath. "What have we got to lose?"

It was hardly the enthusiastic response he'd hoped for. He was not a man who did things by halves. He had little tolerance for people unable or unwilling to take a stand on issues of consequence, and in his view, marriage fell under that heading. But at least she was no longer flatly refusing to consider his proposal and so, conscious of the need not to pressure her into giving more than she felt able to afford just then, he said with matching nonchalance, "Not a thing, Cassandra, but we stand to gain a great deal. Shall we eat?"

"We might as well."

She knelt beside him and laid out the food. "How soon do you think we should do it—get married, I mean?"

"Will a week give you enough time to find a gown and order flowers and send out invitations?"

For the first time since he'd learned of her pregnancy, she actually laughed. "How like a man to ask such a question! Things like that take months to arrange, Benedict. But in our case, it's irrelevant, because I don't want a wedding dress or flowers, or a crowd of well-wishers. A private marriage ceremony before a justice of the peace, with two witnesses, is enough."

"So it is to be a bare-bones formality, with none of the romantic trimmings usually so dear to a woman's heart?"

"Under the circumstances, yes."

"Then how about a honeymoon in Italy, to make up for it?"

"I don't need a honeymoon, either."

Irritation mounting, he was on the point of telling her that if she planned to bring to their marriage the same lack of enthusiasm she showed for her wedding, it was bound to fail miserably. But sensing she needed little encouragement to call the whole thing off, he tempered his annoyance and said as pleasantly as he knew how, "Nevertheless, I would like to give you one. I believe, from the looks of you, that a holiday will do you good. And it so happens that, for reasons to do with my family's business undertakings, I must return shortly to my home in Calabria."

Helping herself to a sliver of chicken breast, she said, "Where's that? You'll have to forgive my ignorance, but I've never visited Italy, so my knowledge of its geography is a bit sketchy. Show me a map, and I can point to major cities like Rome and Milan, but Calabria—"

"Is right down in the toe of the country, across the Strait of Messina from Sicily."

She looked startled. "Isn't Sicily the home of the Mafia?"

"You watch too much television, Cassandra," he said lightly. "I have a beautiful vacation home in Sicily, and it's never once been under attack from the Mafia."

Thoughtfully, she nibbled at a square of melba toast. "Well, I'm sure I'd enjoy seeing it some day, but I'm not convinced this is the time. If you've got family business to attend to, you don't need me traipsing along for the ride. Why don't we put marriage on hold until you come back to the States?"

"And leave you to cope alone with this pregnancy?

Not a chance! I assure you I can deal with my family and still find plenty of time to pay attention to my wife.''

She looked suddenly apprehensive. ''But I'm not sure I *should* be traveling right now. My doctor might not approve.''

''In that case, we'll discuss it with him. If he advises against it, I'll postpone the visit until you feel well enough to make the journey.'' But she continued to look uncertain and, remembering her earlier remark about not having visited Italy, he said, ''What are you really afraid of, *cara?* Is it the idea of flying?''

She shook her head. ''Not at all. It's just that these early weeks of pregnancy have taken such a toll on my energy.''

''All the more reason to take you away from the rigors of work. Calabria is beautiful, Cassandra, a paradise of pristine beaches and clear warm seas. You'll be required to do nothing but relax and let my mother and sisters pamper you.''

''What about your father? What's he going to say about your mixing a honeymoon with business?''

''My father died four years ago.''

''I'm sorry.''

''Don't be,'' he said. ''You had no way of knowing.''

''That's what scares me.'' A frown creased the perfection of her brow. ''One way or another, you've learned quite a bit about me, but I know little about you, and absolutely nothing about the members of your family beyond the fact that they grow a special kind of citrus fruit—bergamot, isn't it?''

''That is it exactly. So you are not as uninformed as you like to pretend.''

''Oh, yes, I am! I wouldn't know a bergamot, if it jumped up and bit me.''

"The bergamot orange is very distinctive. You'll soon learn to recognize it."

"Bergamot...." She lay flat on her back, and ran the word over her tongue, imitating the way he rolled the R. Her hair fanned around her head, a bright halo against the dark green of the grass. "You make it sound so exotic."

"It is a remarkable fruit."

She propped herself up on one elbow to sip at her water, then lay down again and gazed at the canopy of trees overhead. "I remember your telling me, the first time we met, that it's used in the most expensive perfumes, and as a pharmaceutical agent. Is it edible, too?"

"Not in its natural state, but you'll find essence of bergamot used as a flavoring in liquors, tea, and preserved sweets."

"So your family's involved in very big business."

"We make a living."

She slewed a glance at him. The sunlight piercing the branches lent her skin an opalescent gleam and filmed her blue eyes with brilliance, reminding him of the jewelry studded with precious gems created by Calabrian goldsmiths. At another time and in a more private setting, he would have shown her with few words how alluring he found her.

"I'm not asking you how much you're worth, Benedict, if that's what you're thinking," she said soberly. "Just the opposite, in fact. *The Ariel* is a very successful enterprise, and I can well afford to bring up this baby alone. So if you're thinking perhaps I'm marrying you for your money—"

"It never occurred to me that you are, nor is that the reason I proposed. We are marrying because we both wish to do what is best for our child."

She sat up again and helped herself to the grapes. "Just as long as we're both clear on that."

"*Assolutamente!* Would you care for a little cheese with the fruit?"

"You know, I think I would," she said, sounding surprised, and patted her waist lightly. "The fresh air seems to have settled my stomach."

"Or else knowing that the future is more settled has done the trick."

She sampled the cheese thoughtfully a moment, before replying, "Well, I don't mind admitting, the idea of belonging to a large family is rather appealing. I've felt very alone since my mother passed away." She shuffled over to make room for him next to her on his jacket. "Tell me more about your sisters. Are they older or younger than you?"

"Bianca is my age—not surprising, since we're twins!—and is married with two children, a boy, Stefano who's seven, and a girl, Pia, who's three. My brother-in-law Enrico is a lawyer and looks after the legal side of the business, as well as managing our Milano operation—did I mention that we have a few vineyards in Lombardy?"

"No," she said, enchanting him with the lilt of amusement in her voice. "That little detail somehow slipped your mind. But do go on."

"Francesca is twenty-five and still single. She works closely with our mother, running the Calabrian end of things—administration, book-keeping, that kind of thing. We have nearly seventy employees in Calabria, and another thirty in Milano."

"Are you sure there's room for me in such a busy family?"

"They will be overjoyed to welcome you, *cara,*" he

said, hoping it was true. "Every Italian mother wants to see her son produce *un bambino* or two."

"Right now, it's all I can do to manage one and keep track of my appointments." She made a face, a quaint, endearing wrinkling of her elegant nose, and checked the gold fob watch pinned to the lapel of her jacket. "Speaking of which, I have a client meeting in twenty minutes."

"I'll walk you back to the office."

Instead of arguing the point, as she might have done earlier, she merely packed up the remains of their lunch, then brushed the loose grass from his jacket and passed it to him. "I'm glad I wasn't able to talk you out of coming here," she said. "It's a lovely spot, and there's something very soothing in the sound of the waterfall splashing into the pond."

"At my summer home in Sicily," he said, coming up behind her and sliding his arms around her waist, "the sound of the sea lapping on the shore is a night-long lullaby. You will fall asleep with the moon casting stark shadows over the land, and awaken the next morning to golden sunlight and the scent of verbena and rosemary and jasmine."

She leaned against him; let him rest his chin on the crown of her head. "You make it sound idyllic. Can you guarantee that's how our marriage will be?"

"No, *cara*," he murmured, turning her slowly to face him. "The most I can promise is that I will make it the best that it can be. Inevitably, there will be storms, but there will be the calm that follows, and many, many times in between heated by a different passion."

"What kind?" she said, flirting with him from beneath lowered lashes.

"The kind better demonstrated than described in words."

He kissed her then, something he'd been wanting to do ever since she'd stepped out of the elevator almost an hour before. Kissed her long and deeply, and as her mouth softened beneath his, the blood rushed to his loins.

He ached to touch her more intimately; to lay his hand on her belly, where the life within her flourished. His seed, his child…and soon, his wife.

She must have know that he was aroused, yet still she didn't pull away, but instead slipped her hands around his neck, pressed herself closer to him, and whispered unsteadily, "Oh, *that* kind!"

"That," he told her, "is but a token, a promise, if you will, of better things to come."

She drew in a broken sigh. "Suddenly, I wish I didn't have a client waiting for me at the office."

"It's as well that you do," he said, reluctantly putting her from him. "When next we make love, it will be behind closed doors, not in a public park with the ever-present chance of unwelcome visitors intruding on the moment."

She nodded and, with the casual intimacy of a wife or lover, reached up to wipe a fleck of something from the corner of his mouth. "Lipstick," she said, mischief dancing in her eyes. "And it's not your shade at all."

They strolled back along the busy street, the silence between them now easy. "I don't suppose there's any point in my asking you not to work too hard?" he said, as they slowed to a stop next to where a street vendor had set up his flower stall outside her office building.

"Not really. But I promise not to overdo it." She favored him with a brief and lovely smile.

Behind her on the stall, tiny bunches of small, purple flowers echoed the color of her eyes and gave emphasis to the porcelain perfection of her skin. On a whim, he bought one of the sprigs and slipped it behind the pin holding her watch in place.

She gave a muted exclamation of pleasure and dipped her head to sniff the fragrance. "Violets! How did you know I love them?"

"Lucky guess," he said, his attention captured by the slender curve of her neck. "They're small and delicate, like you. *Bella,* like you."

"Sometimes, you say the nicest things." A faint blush accompanied her smile and she touched her fingertips to his hand. "Forgive me having leapt to all the wrong conclusions about last night."

"Consider it forgotten. Focus on the future, instead."

"Yes." She lingered a moment longer, as though reluctant to leave, then wrinkled her nose again in that habit which he found so charming. "I really must go. My client will be waiting."

"We'll talk again," he said. "Very soon."

"Yes." She hesitated, turned away, then at the last moment swung back and kissed his cheek. "Thank you again for lunch," she whispered at his ear, "and...for everything else."

And then she was gone, sweeping gracefully up the marble steps and through the revolving glass door. He stood watching as the dove gray of her suit merged with the colors other people milling about the lobby were wearing. Until her slight figure and blond head were hidden behind larger, anonymous bodies.

He remained there long after the crowd was swallowed up in the elevator, his thoughts troubled. There were serious problems awaiting him in Calabria. Was he being fair to Cassandra in taking her with him, knowing what he did? Yet she was carrying his child so how, in good conscience, could he leave her behind?

He could not. Would not. Which begged another question. How best to break the news to his family that, at a time when so much else was uncertain, he was bringing to the mix a bride who was a stranger to them and to the culture and customs which bound their lives?

CHAPTER FIVE

DINNER was over, the movie finished, the lights dimmed. Cushioned in luxurious leather beside a window in the *Magnifica* section of the Alitalia 767 jet, Cassandra raised her footrest and adjusted her seat to a reclining position. Next to her, her brand-new husband lifted his glance from the report he was studying just long enough to ask, "Comfortable?"

"Mmm-hmm." She tucked the fleecy airline blanket more securely around her legs.

"Think you'll be able to get some rest?"

She nodded and closed her eyes. But sleep, the one thing she never seemed able to get enough of since she'd become pregnant, eluded her. Instead, the events of the last six days raced in living color through her mind like a movie reel come unspooled....

"What did he do to get you to change your mind?" Trish had wondered, when Cassandra returned from her lunch with Benedict and said she'd accepted his proposal.

"Bowled me over with sweet reason, mostly."

"How about dazzled you with his smile? Seduced you with his long-lashed, bedroom eyes?"

"That, too." She'd lifted her lapel, buried her nose again in the damp, sweet-smelling violets. "He can be very convincing when he puts his mind to it."

And very efficient. Leaving her with no time for second thoughts, he'd swung into action. Within seventy-two hours, they'd purchased their marriage license, booked a time for the ceremony to take place at the County Clerk's office, reserved their flight to Italy, and consulted by phone with her obstetrician who, upon hearing of their travel plans, immediately ordered a sonogram, "just to be on the safe side."

"A week or two of rest and relaxation is just what she needs," the doctor affirmed, when they met with him the next afternoon. "However, although the findings of the ultrasound are inconclusive at this stage, the cervix remains a matter of slight concern. We'll reassess the situation when you return but, for the time being, I recommend you refrain from marital relations. Not the kind of news a couple wants to take away with them on a honeymoon, I know, but when a high-risk pregnancy is at stake...."

"This is the first I've heard about there being any kind of risk attached to the pregnancy," Benedict had said, shooting an accusatory look Cassandra's way. "Explain, if you will, Doctor, the possible difficulties my wife will be facing."

Later, over dinner at Pier 39, she'd again suggested they postpone the wedding until such time as they could enjoy a normal honeymoon.

"Absolutely not," Benedict ruled. "Marriage is about more than just sex, Cassandra, and in our case, about a lot more than just you and me. The safety of our baby takes precedence over all else."

His stoic acceptance of the doctor's ruling, added to the brisk, almost businesslike manner with which he treated her thereafter, rendered Trish's parting gift of a diaphanous negligee somewhat pointless, Cassie thought, conscious of the unfamiliar weight of the heavy gold ring on her finger. That it signified marriage was as foreign a concept as the fact that the man sitting next to her was her husband. No matter how many times she told herself, *I am now, for better or worse, Mrs. Benedict Constantino,* the reality didn't sink in. Even yesterday's wedding possessed the elements of a dream fraught with a touch of nightmare.

"I don't even know his birthday!" she'd wailed to Trish. "I don't know his middle name, or what size shirt he wears. I don't know if he likes pajamas or sleeps naked, drives a Mercedes or a pickup truck!"

Trish, ever practical, had said, "Check out the marriage license for his birth date and middle name. As for what he drives, you've only got to look at the man to know it's a Ferrari or a Porsche, and you'll find out soon enough what he wears in bed. Quit fretting about minor details, Cass, and put your shoes on. Ian's bringing the car round, and we don't want to keep the groom or City Hall waiting."

"I can't leave yet," she'd protested, swamped in a rush of panic at what she was about to do. "I think I'm going to be sick again."

"It'll have to wait until after the ceremony," Trish had decreed unsympathetically. "You'll smear your lip gloss and make your mascara run if you throw up now."

But the nausea had persisted. Was with her still, caused not by the pregnancy, or the sudden swooping dip of the aircraft as it hit a patch of turbulence, but by the nervous shock of realizing she'd thrown in her lot with a virtual stranger.

How long before the panic subsided, before being addressed as Signora Constantino stopped taking her by surprise? And how long before Benedict became the man who'd wooed her so persuasively that, within twenty-four hours of his learning she was carrying his child, she'd agreed to marry him?

Beside her, she heard the rustle of papers, the snap of his briefcase closing, the sibilant whisper of the soft leather seat as his body made itself comfortable for the night. His elbow nudged hers, remained there, warm and solid. She felt, rather than heard his breathing become slow and relaxed.

Alert for a sign that he'd fallen asleep, she waited five minutes…ten. The man in the row behind snored loudly enough to be heard over the drone of the jet engines, but not Benedict. If he slept, and she thought from the utter stillness of his body that he must, it was with the same unruffled competence that he did everything else.

At last, cautiously, she turned her head, and opened her eyes. Yes, he was sleeping, sprawled elegantly in his seat with his hands clasped loosely in his lap, which left her free to examine at leisure the strong, clean lines of his profile.

He looked just as he had the previous morning, when they exchanged their wedding vows: a study in charcoal and bronze, iron-jawed and unsmiling. Thoroughly masculine, thoroughly composed. No untoward dreams would disturb his rest. They wouldn't dare!

His lashes, thick and luxuriant enough to make a woman weep with envy, smudged dark against his high cheekbones. His hair, usually tamed to within an inch of its life, lay slightly rumpled across his brow. And his mouth…?

She studied the patrician curve of his lips and her throat went dry. But a flush of heat settled between her legs as if *that* part of her body had stolen all her moisture to ease its sudden ache.

No question about it! She knew more about his mouth—how it tasted and felt, and what it could do to drive her crazy with desire—than she did about any other part of him.

What sort of a basis did *that* make for a solid marriage?

She was still pondering the thought when, without a flicker of warning, his lashes swept up and she found herself trapped in the unblinking enigma of his dark eyes.

"Well?" he said, his voice low and commanding. "Will I do?"

Taking refuge in the absurdly obvious, she said, "I thought you were sleeping."

The corner of his mouth lifted in the ghost of a smile. "Your kind of intense, unswerving scrutiny could raise the dead, Cassandra, let alone awaken a sleeping man. But you haven't answered my question. *Will* I do, or are you already regretting having married me?"

"You're very handsome," she allowed. "Very aristocratic-looking, and very...decent. A woman would have to be crazy to regret being your wife."

"And at this moment, you're having serious doubts about your sanity, yes?"

She wanted to wrench her gaze away, but found she couldn't. Found herself compelled by the candor in his eyes to respond in kind. "I admit, at the moment, I'm feeling somewhat overwhelmed."

"I wish I could reassure you," he said, "but that's something only time can achieve. The best I can do is tell you that I am exactly as I've presented myself to you: a man bound by honor and tradition to abide by his marriage vows and provide well for his wife and baby. Furthermore, I consider myself fortunate in the extreme to have found a woman of such beauty and intelligence to be the mother of my child."

He reached across the console dividing their seats and touched the sleeve of her wedding outfit, a deep aquamarine silk knit dress with a knee-length skirt and matching jacket, which she and Trish had shopped for during their lunch hour, earlier in the week. She'd worn it again today because it was both comfortable and stylish, and she wanted to look her best when she met his family. "We didn't have an elaborate wedding," he said, "but you made a beautiful bride, nevertheless."

"I hope your family thinks so. You never did tell me how they received the news, when you phoned to tell them you were bringing back a wife. Were they pleased?"

"They responded much as I expected they would."

The ambiguity of his reply was not lost on her. Uneasily, she said, "That doesn't sound very promising."

He gave her hand a perfunctory pat, as if she were a child incapable of understanding the complexities of the grown-up world he occupied. "Leave me to worry about my family, Cassandra, and concentrate only of giving birth to a healthy, full-term baby."

"Don't brush me off like that, Benedict," she said sharply. "If this marriage of ours is to stand any sort of chance at all, the very least you can do is address my concerns, just as you expect me to address yours."

He expelled a sigh, though whether of annoyance or fatigue she couldn't tell. "Very well. It's fair to say my family was surprised."

"And happy for you?"

"I didn't ask them."

More disquieted by the second, she said, "Why not?"

"Because the call was brief, and the connection poor. We will be in Italy only a matter of a week or two. That being the case, my family's happiness, or lack thereof, is scarcely relevant.''

Although he answered straightforwardly enough, she knew there was more to it than he was telling her. It showed in the sudden tightening of his mouth, the way he shifted impatiently in his seat.

"They don't approve, do they?" she said. "They don't want you bringing home a bride."

"What does it matter, Cassandra? *I* wanted it, which leaves them with little choice but to accept you." The almost clinical detachment with which he spoke turned his meager crumbs of comfort to poison. "You and I are, as our French friends would say, a *fait accompli,* and there's not a damned thing anyone can do or say to change that."

Crushed, she turned her head and gazed bleakly out at the star-spattered sky beyond the porthole. Any other husband en route to introducing his new wife to his family would have said, *They'll adore you, just as I do.* But unlike most bridegrooms, Benedict was not besotted with his new wife,

Nor did he pretend to be. "I wanted *it,*" he'd said, meaning "the marriage." Not, "I wanted *you.*" And the reason, as she'd known from the outset, was that she was pregnant with his child. So why the sudden stinging hurt, the acute sense that she'd been robbed?

"Will the whole family be meeting us in Milan?" she asked, praying they would not. Nine hours of jet travel, no matter how comfortable the accommodation on board or forgiving the outfit she was wearing, did not leave any woman looking her best, and it seemed she already had her work cut out to make a favorable impression.

"No. Only Bianca and Enrico will be there. As I already explained, there's no direct flight from New York to my family home, and Milan lies almost a thousand kilometers north of Calabria. It makes no sense for my mother and Francesca to cover such a distance when they'll meet you anyway the following day." He yawned and closed his eyes. "Get some sleep, Cassandra. You've had a hectic couple of days, what with flying from San Francisco to New York yesterday, and now this. You must be exhausted."

Exhausted, Benedict? she thought, turning her face away from him and refusing to allow another hormonally induced rash of tears to take hold. *How about discouraged, offended, and resentful? Just who do these relatives of yours think they are, to judge me unfavorably before they've even laid eyes on me?*

"Does Cassandra not speak any Italian?" Bianca asked.

"A word or two—*ciao, grazie, arrivederci.* Common, everyday words only. Enough to be polite but not enough to carry on a conversation."

"Benedict, are you mad to have brought her here at this time? You know how she'll be received by our mother."

He shrugged and kept on walking. The evening was mild for late March, the parklike grounds of his sister's country home, an hour's drive from the city, a feast for the eyes with its tree-shaded paths and long sweeps of lawn rimmed with flower beds just beginning to bloom. "Leave me to enjoy tonight, Bianca. Tomorrow is soon enough to worry about our mother. Regardless of how she might react to my marriage, you know I'll deal with her."

"Not easily, for something this momentous, and especially not at this time." She slipped an affectionate arm through his. "I didn't want to burden you with bad news when you phoned to tell us you were getting married, but she's becoming more irrational by the day, and I'm afraid the situation's even worse now than it was when last you were here.''

''I don't see how that's possible. There were only a handful of people left working the land then, and I paid them handsomely to stay on the job, with the promise of a further bonus when I returned.''

''And as far as I know, only a very few have remained loyal. The rest are gone. Even worse, the dissatisfaction has spread to the kitchen and household staff. Sergio walked out at the weekend, which meant his wife and daughter went with him. Then, two days ago, Guido left. The only one still there is Speranza, and how much abuse she's taking as a result isn't something I like to dwell on.''

''That's completely unacceptable!'' Speranza was past seventy, had been with his family since well before Benedict was born, and would, he knew, die on the job before she'd abandon the family she loved as if it were her own. For her to be attending to her own work and taking on that of four others, all considerably younger, was not to be tolerated.

''Of course it is!'' Bianca gave a troubled sigh. ''How did this happen so fast, Benedict? A year ago, everything was running smoothly, everyone was happy. Now, we have a full-scale disaster on our hands, and I dread to think how we'll manage when harvesting the bergamot begins again in October. Unless you can turn things around quickly, we'll default on some of our most important client contracts. Should that happen, not only will we stand to lose money but, far worse, our reputation, too.''

"It won't happen," he promised. "I'll handle everything."

"On your honeymoon? I don't see the two mixing well!"

"It's a working holiday. Cassandra understands that."

"But she looks frail and anxious, this little wife of yours, and sad, too. And you…you're not glowing with happiness, either. Shouldn't you be concentrating on each other, and not business?"

"We're both tired, that's all. The last week's been hectic, what with making travel arrangements and then the wedding."

"Is there a reason that it took place so suddenly?"

He blew out a long, uneven breath. "Oh, yes! She's pregnant."

"Dio!" Her face a study in shocked exasperation, Bianca pulled her arm free and planted herself in his path. "Benedict, how could you have allowed—?"

"I know, I know! You expected better of me. I expected better of myself. But things are what they are, and I have to make the best of them."

"You're not in love with Cassandra?"

"I am drawn to her. She wouldn't be carrying my child otherwise."

"Does our mother know?"

"About the baby, no. Nor do I plan to tell her until I see how things go. But I'm confiding in you, Bianca, because we've always been close and I know you'll accept Cassandra without censure."

"Of course! She's a sweet and lovely woman. I can see why you'd be attracted to her, and I welcome her as my sister. But Benedict…" She looked away and he knew from the way that she lapsed into silence that she was deeply concerned.

"But I've disappointed you." His smile was part amusement, part regret. "I've fallen off my pedestal and shown myself to be as human as the next man,"

"Oh, it's not that! You're my brother and I'd never judge you." She let out another sigh. "But the difficulties I spoke of at home in the south...well, they don't end with our mother."

"You mean, there's more, and it's worse? I don't see how that's possible!"

"I'm afraid it is. Apparently, those few retainers who've remained loyal to the family are being bullied by defectors with blood contacts in the Aspromonte." She cast him a worried look. "We both know the kind of danger that presents, Benedict. We're dealing with *la 'ndrangheta,* something which never would have happened in our father's day because he would never have hired such ruffians in the first place."

Benedict was no coward, but this latest revelation gave rise to a thread of uneasiness which ran too close to fear for his peace of mind. The threat from *la 'ndrangheta*—the local Mafia, whose chief source of income was kidnapping members of wealthy families and extorting huge ransoms for their safe return—was not something to be taken lightly. Lawless and without conscience, they lived in the wild mountainous region of the interior of the province and were answerable to no one but themselves.

"If that's the case, we have a critical situation on our hands," he said, again questioning how wise he'd been to insist on having Cassandra accompany him on this trip. "To expect that they'll feel themselves bound by the moral dictates which govern the rest of our lives is unrealistic. If vengeance is an issue, they'll deal with it in ways we can't begin to imagine."

"Exactly. We grew up hearing the stories—about the people who disappear and are never heard from again, the vendettas carried out—and nothing's changed. I'm afraid for Francesca, as well as for our mother." She tucked her hand more firmly under his arm. "And I'm afraid for you, as well, Benedict."

"Don't be," he said. "I can take care of myself, and Francesca and our mother, too. But Cassandra is another matter. If the situation at the palazzo strikes me as too risky, I'd like to know I can send her to you for refuge."

"Of course! As often, and for as long as you need."

"Thank you." He stopped and squeezed her hand. "I've always been able to rely on you."

"We've relied on each other, *caro*, and that doesn't change just because we're both now married. We're family. We always will be."

They resumed walking. Dusk had fallen, and lamplight shone behind many of the windows fronting the house. But looking up, Benedict located the room where Cassandra waited in the wide guest bed, and saw that it lay in darkness. Did that mean she was asleep?

He hoped so. He wasn't sure he could face her again tonight and not have his concern show.

Hidden by a fold in the filmy drapes, Cassie looked down on the gardens. Earlier, peacocks had strutted across the lawn and the children playing hide-and-seek. But now, with the moon rising in the east, the garden was deserted except for the figures of her husband and his twin strolling back along the night-shadowed path to the balustraded forecourt below her window. They were enviably at ease in each other's company—and so oblivious of her that she might as well not exist.

Not that she hadn't been well received by his sister

and her husband. When they'd met at Malpensa airport, Bianca Constantino Manzini had folded Cassie in a hug, kissed her on both cheeks, and said in charmingly accented but otherwise perfect English, "I am so happy to meet you, Cassandra, and so thrilled that my brother has found someone with whom to share his life. Welcome to Milano and our family!"

Equally warm, Enrico had echoed his wife's sentiments, which ought to have reassured Cassandra. And perhaps it would have, had Benedict not grown correspondingly more remote, more preoccupied. But immediately upon arrival at the Manzini residence, he'd disappeared without a word into Enrico's home office, and left his wife to fend for herself.

"Family business," Bianca had explained apologetically, noticing Cassie's dismay at being so soon abandoned among strangers. "Always with this family, the business must be attended to first, and then we play. So, *cara*, while our men pore over legal documents and international import regulations, come and meet my children. They're so eager to greet their new aunt, and you're here for such a short spell this time, that I kept my son home from school today so that he could make the most of your visit."

As she spoke, she'd led the way to a large sunny room at the rear of the house, where a boy worked on a model aircraft at a table, and a girl played on the floor with a doll house. Both of them dark and beautiful like their mother, they stopped what they were doing and stood politely during the formal introductions.

"Hello," the boy had murmured shyly, shaking Cassie's hand. "You are welcoming to *Italia*."

"Stefano's been practicing saying that in English ever since Benedict phoned to let us know he was bringing

you to meet us,'' Bianca told her in an amused aside.
''I'm afraid, though, that he still doesn't have it quite
right.''

''Never mind,'' Cassie had replied, completely won
over by the boy's smile. ''His English is a whole lot
better than my Italian. He puts me to shame.''

The girl, Pia, unwilling to remain in her brother's
shade, rattled off a stream of Italian of which only *Ciao!*
meant anything to Cassie. But she understood what was
expected of her when the child tugged at her hand and
pulled her over to admire the doll's house which, with
its elaborate facade and rooms full of exquisite furniture,
was truly a work of art.

''A gift from Benedict,'' Bianca said. ''He's a very
indulgent uncle and will be, I'm sure, an equally indulgent husband.''

Perhaps not, if his recent attitude was anything to go
by, Cassie thought now, letting the drapes fall back into
place as Benedict and Bianca disappeared from view,
although his apparent devotion to his niece and nephew
boded well for his own child. But then, she already knew
that because, as he was so fond of saying, ''The baby
comes first.''

Down below, a door thudded closed and voices, one
deeply resonant as only a man's could be, the other fem-
inine and full of laughter, drifted up from the entrance
hall in a vivacious burst of rapid-fire Italian. Opening the
bedroom door a crack, Cassie caught the occasional
word—*domani…bambini,* and her own name, Cassandra.

Beyond that, she hadn't the first clue what her husband and sister-in-law were talking about, and promised
herself that, tomorrow, she'd buy an Italian phrase book
at the airport, and study it during the short flight to

Calabria. Hopefully, if she memorized a few common expressions—*I'm very pleased to meet you. How are you? You have a lovely home*—it might persuade her new mother-in-law to look upon her more favorably.

And Benedict? Would her effort to absorb something of his culture and background move him to treat her with the kind of warmth he'd initially shown when he sought her out again in San Francisco? Or was his present courteous reserve all she had to look forward to, now that he'd achieved his ambition and made her his wife?

Oh, he was kind enough, in an abstract sort of way, but somewhere between his asking her to marry him, and her saying "I do," the sexual electricity which had charged their every encounter had flickered and died. Beyond a sedate kiss on the cheek, an impersonal hand at her elbow to help her cross the street or climb out of a car, he made no attempt to touch her anymore.

At first, she'd put down the change in him to his having too many other matters occupying his attention, too many demands on his time. She'd told herself that, once they'd left all the rush behind, and it was just the two of them in Italy, he'd be his former self again and the old attraction would resurface.

But it hadn't happened. If anything, with each passing hour, he became more…*absentmindedly paternalistic.* And she hated it!

The moon, now fully risen above the trees, cast a pale and melancholy light over the room, and reduced the warm wood of the elegant furniture to a chill, tomblike gray. And she, on her supposed honeymoon, sat propped up by pillows, alone in the wide, wrought-iron bed.

Too drained to flick on the reading lamp and lose herself in the paperback novel lying in her lap, too homesick for the familiar comfort of her own house and friends, and too at odds with her tangled emotions to take refuge in sleep, she stared into the semi-darkness.

How long she remained like that, utterly motionless, utterly miserable, she neither knew nor cared. At some level, she was aware of the house gradually sinking into peaceful silence, but it could have been hours or only minutes before she heard the well-oiled *snick* of the door opening, and saw Benedict's tall figure on the threshold, silhouetted by the soft glow of a night-light in the upper hall.

Quietly, he closed the door, and picked his way across the floor, clearly intending to shut himself in the adjoining dressing room so as not to disturb her. But she, anticipating just such a move, announced coldly, "It's quite all right to turn on the light, Benedict. Contrary to your express command, I am not sleeping."

Startled into dropping the shoes he'd been carrying, he let out a smothered exclamation, and groped for the switch on the bedside lamp. "Then why the devil are you sitting here in the dark?"

She blinked in the sudden bright glare. "What does it look like?" she said. "I'm waiting for my husband to come to bed, the way all brides do on their honeymoon. Or isn't that the custom in Italy?"

CHAPTER SIX

HE MADE a big production of removing his jacket and tie, and hanging them in the wardrobe. "If I'd known you were still wide-awake—"

"You'd have done what?" she snapped, glaring at his back. "Stayed here to keep me company, instead of going for an evening stroll with your sister?"

He spun back to face her, a frown creasing his brow. "I wasn't aware you knew we'd gone out. Were you watching us?"

"I *saw* you, which isn't quite the same thing. And I wondered if there was a reason you sent me off to bed, instead of asking me to join you."

"Cassandra," he said, standing at the foot of the bed, and adopting that reasonable I-know-what's-best-for-you tone she was beginning to loathe, "you were fading so noticeably over dinner that it simply didn't occur to me to ask you to come with us."

"I'm pregnant, Benedict, not terminally ill. And I'm old enough to decide for myself when I need to retire for the night."

"Fine!" He shrugged, removed his cuff links, and took his time rolling his shirtsleeves midway up his forearms. "Forgive me for caring enough about your welfare to give a damn! In future, do as you please."

"I intend to," she informed him. "And right now, it pleases me to discover why you're more interested in acting like my guardian than my husband. A week ago, you couldn't get enough of my company. Now, you're so busy keeping your distance, I'm beginning to feel like Typhoid Mary.''

His mouth fell open and for a long, silent moment, he simply stared at her. Then he leaned against the dresser and let fly with a great, rich burst of merriment unlike anything she'd heard from him before. ''I don't recall ever having met such a person,'' he finally managed to splutter. ''Do I take it she's not particularly nice to be near?''

''Stop being trying to be cute, Benedict! It doesn't suit you. And while you're at it, you can stop guffawing, as well, and just give me a straight answer.''

He stroked his chin and made a pitiful effort to keep a straight face, but when he spoke, his voice still quivered with suppressed laughter. ''I'm trying, but if only you could see yourself, *cara,* perched there among your mountain of pillows, looking for all the world like a queen reprimanding a wayward subject.''

To her horror and chagrin, tears overflowed her eyes and leaked down her face. ''I'm glad one of us finds this amusing.''

''Ah, Cassandra…!'' In one swift stride, he came to her and perched on the edge of the mattress. ''Where is all this nonsense coming from? If you wanted to come with Bianca and me this evening, all you had to do was say so.''

''I didn't, not really,'' she sniffed, knowing she was being absurd and hating the fact that she had so little control of her emotions these days. ''I'd probably have been in the way.''

''Not so. Bianca was telling me how much she likes you.'' He cupped her jaw, his touch warm and tender. ''Has someone else made you feel unwelcome here?''

''No. Bianca and Enrico couldn't be kinder, their children are a delight, and their house staff very helpful. But let's face it, Benedict, for all that they're trying not to let it show, your sister and brother-in-law are reeling with shock at your showing up with a wife, and hardly know what to make of our marriage. And frankly, in light of your growing indifference toward me, nor do I.''

He reared back, shock evident in every feature. ''You believe I'm indifferent to you?''

''Maybe not,'' she said, on a miserable sigh. ''Maybe it's just me, overreacting again. All I know is that I'm a stranger in a strange land, miles away from anyone who really cares about me.''

''*I* care, Cassandra.''

''Only because I'm pregnant.''

''Not only because of that,'' he said, leaning forward to capture her hands. ''And if you think the reason I'm keeping my distance is that I don't want to be near you, then you're not just pregnant, you're hopelessly naive as well.''

''In that case, come to bed,'' she begged, hanging on to him for dear life. ''Don't let this be a repeat of two nights ago.''

He grew very still. ''I'm not sure I understand you.''

''I might be naive, Benedict, but I'm not delusional. I went to bed alone on our wedding night, awoke after midnight to find myself still alone, and had the same thing happen again, the next morning.''

''I didn't want to disturb you,'' he said. ''You'd had a very long day, and before that, a very busy week. When I came to the bedroom, you were sleeping so deeply that I thought it best if I stayed on the sofa in my study.''

''Well, I'm not sleeping now.''

"But you should be. Your doctor wouldn't be pleased to know you're defying his instructions."

"He wouldn't be pleased to know I'm stressed out because my husband's ignoring me, either!"

His gaze burned into hers. He was not a man given to indecision, yet at that moment she saw torment in his eyes and she quaked inside at what it might signify. Did he find her repugnant, with her heavy breasts and subtle thickening at the waist, and endless bouts of nausea? Or had the rashness of their decision to marry finally hit home, and he was horrified at the commitment he'd made?

Whatever the cause, eventually he lifted his shoulders in mute surrender and disappeared into the dressing room. Shortly after, she heard the door to the en suite bathroom close, and the sound of water running in the shower. When he returned to the bedroom some fifteen minutes later, she'd turned off the reading lamp and lay beneath the lightweight duvet, taut with a mixture of anticipation and dread.

The moon, peeping through the window, illuminated his path to the bed. Without a word, he climbed in beside her and lay on his back, motionless, with his hands clasped behind his head. On the nightstand, a small gilt clock marked the passing time...*tick...tick...tick...*

Only a few inches of mattress separated his body from hers, yet it might as well have been an abyss, and she couldn't bear it. Whispering his name, she turned to him and laid her hand on his bare chest. His skin was cool and smooth beneath a dusting of hair. Dark against the ghostly white of the bed linen. Sculpted by underlying muscle.

But except for the steady beat of his heart and the

slow rise and fall of his breathing, he might as well have been dead, so unmoved was her by her touch.

Her voice awash with tearful pleading, she said again, "Benedict, I feel so alone!"

"You're not alone, Cassandra. I'm here."

"Then hold me. Let me feel your warmth."

He unclasped his hands and slipped a wary, avuncular arm around her shoulders. Starving for his touch, she burrowed against him and pressed her mouth to the side of his neck, savoring the scent of soap and man.

Immediately, he pulled away. "Stop that!" he muttered, his voice strangled.

"Why?" she said. "Don't you want me?"

"So badly I can taste it," he replied. "But I can't have you. Not now. Not yet. You can do your worst to tempt me, Cassandra, but I will do nothing to endanger your pregnancy."

"But we can touch, can't we?" She splayed her fingers over his chest again, circled the raised point of his nipples. "We can caress. We can kiss."

"I kiss you," he said. "I kissed you good night before you came upstairs."

"Not the way you did before. Not as if you can't get enough of me." She raised herself up on one elbow and leaned over him. "Not like this," she said, lowering her mouth to his and sweeping her tongue over his lower lip.

Roughly, he turned his head aside and swore—at least, she supposed he did, given the stifled violence in his tone, even though she didn't understand the words he used. "You go too far, Cassandra!" he said hoarsely. "Let it be enough that we're married!"

"I can't," she said, encouraged by the betraying, savage rasp of his breathing. "What if you grow tired of being a husband in name only?"

"Do you think me an animal, that I can't control my carnal appetite?"

She stroked her hand over his stomach, pushed down the briefs he wore, and with the tip of her finger traced the curve of skin where the top of his thigh met his hip. "No," she said, smiling a little at his dignified usage of English because it bore no relation whatsoever to the highly indecorous response of his body. "I think you are a man who deserves better than to be lying in bed with a wife who can't pleasure you."

"Cassandra, I'm begging you…!"

He was big and hard and heavy. Pulsing and alive. *Alive for her…!*

"Be quiet, Benedict," she said gently, and lowering her head, closed her lips around his penis.

He tasted divine, and she wanted all of him—everything he had to give. And so she took, repeatedly drawing him deep into her mouth.

He knotted his fingers in her hair.

Groaned and shuddered.

Arched up to meet her.

Cursed her. Forbade her. Threatened her.

Fought as only a man of iron will could fight—until his soul lay shredded within him, and his strength gave out.

Only then, when nothing he invoked deterred her, did he concede defeat and, with a wrenching involuntary spasm that shook his entire body, spilled into her mouth.

"So much for taking a long, cold, unpleasant shower before joining you in bed," he said grimly, when his heart rate diminished enough that he could speak again. "I hope you're satisfied with what you accomplished."

She raised her head and looked at him. His eyes glittered in the moonlight and sweat gleamed on his skin. "Oh, yes, Benedict," she said, dutifully, the way a compliant wife should. "Are you?"

He swore again, the same thing he'd said before, but uttered mellifluously this time. Like music; like a love song.

He stretched out his hand. "Come here," he said, and drew her up to lie close beside him. "And listen to me. This is not how it should be between a man and a woman, that the pleasure is all his while she receives nothing."

"Whoever made up that rule didn't know what he was talking about."

"Nevertheless, it is the Italian way."

A warm and lovely lassitude crept over her, leaving her limbs heavy and her spirit more peaceful than it had felt in days. "Then stop being so Italian," she purred. "Just say 'thank you' and accept the fact that, sometimes, giving pleasure to her man is all the reward a woman needs."

She sensed his smile. Heard it in his murmured, *"Mi scusi, cara. Grazie, e buona notte!"*

Cassie thought herself well-prepared to meet her mother-in-law. Throughout the one and a half hour flight from Milan to Calabria, she'd memorized *Buono giorno, Signora Constantino. Lieto di conoscerla*—which, according to her phrase book, amounted pretty much to, "Hello, Mrs. Constantino. Lovely to meet you."

By the time the plane touched down at Lamezia Terme, she was confident that, when the moment presented itself, she could recite her greeting with reasonable fluency.

She might as well have studied Swahili, for all the good it did her!

First of all, the forty kilometer drive from the airport to Benedict's family home, though passing through exquisite countryside, meant taking a narrow, twisting coastal road which at times seemed to hang by a thread from the steep cliffs hugging the shore. As if that alone wasn't enough to sweep her mind clear of everything but white-knuckled terror, his car was no conservative family sedan but a low-slung red Lamborghini Diablo designed for speed. And that, she quickly surmised, clinging to the edge of her seat and praying they'd arrive alive, was clearly the chief reason he'd chosen it, because he drove with the death-defying disregard of a man competing in the Indy 500.

However, apart from a short stop to buy bottled water in one of the villages they passed through, they completed the journey without incident, and with little in the way of conversation. Although his manner toward Cassie was warmer, he appeared preoccupied and when they arrived at his family home, Cassie could well see why.

Unlike Bianca's light and airy residence, the Palazzo Constantino was a great gothic heap of a place, with high walls and narrow windows. Accessed by an electronic gate, it sat within a vast, rather unkempt garden overlooking the sea, its facade so forbidding that Cassie's first thought was that it looked more like a medieval prison than a home.

Not a soul came out to welcome them as the car passed beneath a stone arch and snarled to a stop in an inner courtyard bound on all four sides by the palazzo walls, nor did Benedict seem to find this strange. ''I'll bring in the luggage later,'' he said, ushering her into a vast stone-paved entrance hall. "Let's get you settled first."

Outside, the sun shone from a cloudless sky, but nothing of its warmth penetrated that cold interior. Nor did it touch the throaty contralto of the woman who suddenly appeared from the shadow of the massive central staircase dominating the area. Although she spoke in her native tongue, her displeasure was unmistakable and sent a chill of foreboding up Cassie's spine.

It had no such effect on Benedict. Leading Cassie forward, he said in English, "I have brought my wife to meet you, Mother, and she does not speak Italian. And so, in her presence, neither will we. Cassandra, may I present to you my mother, Elvira."

Before Cassie could pull herself together enough to recite her little speech, Elvira Constantino stepped closer, skimmed her in a disparaging head-to-toe gaze, and turned to Benedict. "So, *le mio figlio*," she drawled, her tone insultingly close to a sneer, "this is the woman of whom you spoke on the telephone."

Not about to show her dismay at such a reception, Cassie boldly stared back. When they'd stopped to buy their water, she'd noticed black-clad women, with shawls covering their heads, sitting in house doorways, knitting or weaving, and chattering animatedly among themselves. Many had stopped what they were doing long enough to smile broadly, and wave a greeting.

In common with them, Elvira also wore black, but there the similarity ended. Not for her the villagers' simple cotton or friendly greeting, but attitude to spare, all dressed up in Italian haute couture at its most elegant. Her tailored suit of finely corded silk was exquisite, her shoes fashioned from leather so soft they appeared to caress her feet, rather than encase them.

Her nails were lacquered and she wore gem-studded rings on the fingers of both hands. Gold hoops swung from her ears and her hair, a magnificent shining ebony mass with not a hint of silver, was swept up in a classic chignon to showcase her smooth olive complexion and aristocratic features.

Although her dark eyes snapped with hostility and her mouth curved in scorn for the pale, pathetic specimen her son had landed on her doorstep, she had been a great beauty in her youth and remained an indisputably handsome woman.

"This is my *wife* and her name is *Cassandra*," Benedict repeated in a tone that, had he addressed Cassie in such a way, would have left her withering on the spot. "And I expect you to make her feel at home here, Elvira."

"I am no miracle worker," the woman returned disdainfully. "Calabria is for Calabrians and it's well-known that foreigners do not adapt easily to our way of life. But…" She lifted her elegant shoulders as though importuning the gods to reward her well for her charity. "I will do my best."

Her immediate "best" was to lean forward and touch her cheek to her daughter-in-law's, and it was all Cassie could do not to shrink from the contact. A corpse possessed more warmth!

"So…" She stepped away again and subjected Cassie to another sweeping survey. "You would like to repair yourself before we share a little refreshment, yes?"

Cassie had taken great pains with her appearance that morning, choosing fine wool slacks and a tunic top in hyacinth-blue, with ivory low-heeled shoes which were every bit as elegant in their way as Elvira's black pumps. Nevertheless, she quailed under that contemptuous stare and, feeling suddenly as dusty and travel-stained as a stray picked up off the side of the road, muttered lamely, "Thank you. That would be very nice."

Dismissing her with a languid blink of her magnificent dark eyes, Elvira stepped to the wall and pulled on a chain which resulted in a bell sounding distantly, somewhere in the bowels of the building. "I have arranged for you and your wife to stay in the blue suite on the third floor, Benedict. It offers more space than your usual room," she said. "Speranza will show her the way."

"Oh, that's not necessary," Cassie began. The idea of being shipped off with a stranger, to some remote part of this mausoleum, had all the makings of a horror movie she'd just as soon not be taking part in. "I can wait until Benedict's ready to go up, as well."

But her words fell on deaf ears. "That will not be for quite some time. There are matters I must discuss with my son which hold no interest for you," Elvira informed her bluntly, and proceeded to match action to her words by interspersing herself between Cassie and Benedict, and making her way toward a room opening to the right of the staircase. "The problems we spoke of last week, Benedict," she said, tossing the words over her shoulder, "have intensified. We must take immediate action to prevent any further disruption to our operations."

"Bianca mentioned as much," he replied, following his mother, and Cassie knew from his distracted expression that he'd already relegated his wife to the back of his mind.

Well, what else did she expect? Hadn't Bianca warned her, *Always with this family, the business must be attended to first?*

But recognizing the truth of the statement did little to

mitigate the sense of abandonment sweeping over her as she stood alone in that chill, unfriendly place. Never before in her life had she felt so utterly and completely irrelevant.

The blue suite turned out to be a dim and cavernous pair of overfurnished rooms, with cold marble floors, heavy, dark draperies at the windows, and a vaguely damp smell permeating the air. It lay at the end of a long corridor on the third floor, and Cassie feared for the poor soul commandeered to show her the way.

Speranza was an ancient little lady, doubled over with age, arthritis, or a combination of both, and how she managed the stairs so nimbly was nothing short of extraordinary. She spoke not a word of English, but her eyes, though sharply observant, were kind, and her smile genuine as she pointed out *il balcone* off the sitting area, the massive iron four-poster in the bedroom, and finished off the grand tour with the en suite bathroom.

"Il bagno," she declared proudly, flinging open the door with a flourish. *"Moderno, si?"*

"Si," Cassie agreed, although there was no shower stall and the deep, claw-foot tub and washbasin, with their large brass faucets, bore the stamp of an earlier era. But the toilet and bidet were of more recent vintage, and the towels, folded neatly on a glass shelf, thick and luxurious. *"Grazie."*

"Prego!" Nodding and smiling encouragingly, the old woman poked herself in the chest. *"Sono Speranza,"* she declared.

"You're Speranza?"

"Si, si!" Eyebrows raised inquiringly, she pointed at Cassie. *"Come si chiama?"*

"Cassie," she replied, guessing she'd been asked her name.

"Cass-ee. *Eccellente!*" Grinning approval, Speranza patted her arm, then shuffled back to her duties below stairs, leaving a vast and lonely silence in her wake.

Were the other rooms on this floor occupied, or were she and Benedict to live up here in splendid isolation, Cassie wondered, drawing back the draperies in the bedroom, and gazing down at the courtyard.

To her surprise, she saw Benedict there, hauling their luggage out of the car, with Elvira standing close by. Gesticulating wildly, she spoke to him in rapid, staccato bursts, and although her words were indistinguishable, her voice, hoarse with urgency—or anger—floated clearly up the chimneylike enclosure formed by the surrounding walls.

Eventually, Benedict answered with something short and imperative which stopped her in midstream. She took a step back from him, held a hand to each side of her perfectly coiffed head, and rocked it back and forth as if in great pain. After observing her in silence a moment, he spoke again, less harshly this time, but the genuine affection Cassie had witnessed between him and his sister the evening before was markedly absent.

Elvira spat a reply and turned to stare across the courtyard which lay cast in shadow already, even though the sky remained a clear and tranquil blue. A still, black figure in a gray and somber setting, she'd have resembled the evil witch in a fairy tale had she been bent and gnarled with age. Instead, she stood tall and regally proud, every line in her body proclaiming her a woman who'd make a formidable enemy for anyone who, in any way, thwarted her ambitions.

Suddenly, as if sensing she was being observed, she

tilted her gaze up to the window three floors above. Even though she stood some forty or more feet away, the rage in her eyes was so apparent that Cassie recoiled. Not normally given to superstition, she experienced such a chilling prescience of tragedy that her skin puckered with dread.

Her movement did not go unnoticed. Elvira's joyless mouth widened in a smile as purely malevolent as anything Cassie ever hoped to encounter.

CHAPTER SEVEN

ALTHOUGH the face was the same, the virago who'd alternately railed and sniped at Benedict for the last hour bore no resemblance to the mother he'd known as a child. Nor, for that matter, was she anything like the woman she'd been a year ago.

There was a malice in her now which soured everything she touched, including her relationship with him. He might have attributed the change to grief at losing her husband, except that she'd been widowed for four years. Unless she was suffering a delayed reaction, he had every reason to suppose her period of mourning was long past.

"Understand this," he told her, putting an end to her ranting by striding from the office to the rear of the main hall, and claiming the suitcases still at the foot of the stairs. "I will tolerate none of your nonsense toward Cassandra. Accept that she is my wife."

"Never!" Elvira vowed, trailing after him. "You were meant to marry Giovanna."

"That was your dream, Elvira, not mine."

His mother's voice inched a notch closer to outright hysteria. "You do not love this American! There is no passion in your eyes when you look at her! You are a red-blooded man, Benedict—a Constantino—and she will never succeed in filling your needs!"

No? Recalling the night before, he had to curb a smile. Taking his silence to mean he agreed, Elvira continued her harangue. "Why have you shackled yourself to a woman so pale and uninteresting?"

He debated telling her about the pregnancy, and decided to stick with his first instinct to keep the news for a more auspicious time. He and Cassandra were there for only a short while. Why cause more friction than already existed? It would be different if they planned to move permanently to Italy.

"You see?" his mother gloated. "You can't answer, because you know I speak the truth. You've married an adventuress who will bring you nothing but grief, when you could have taken for your wife a fine Calabrian woman who adores you and understands the role required of her. What sort of sense does that make?"

"Relationships don't have to make sense in order to work, Mother," he said, starting up the stairs with the luggage. "Let it be enough that Cassandra and I are committed to one another. If you can't deal with that, at least have the good grace to put up a pleasant front for the time we're here, otherwise you'll leave me with no choice but to take my wife back to the United States immediately—which I'm perfectly prepared to do, and which will then leave you and Francesca to sort out, on your own, the mess you've made of things here."

With a stunning reversal, she latched onto his arm. "When did you become so cruel that you'd speak to me so coldly? You were never this way before. What's changed you?"

"I might ask you the same question."

"I am your mother," she said, and for a moment, with her tone and demeanor, she was. "Benedict, I beg you, in the name of your dead father, do not humiliate me by leaving, when you are so badly needed here!"

Despite all her earlier, irrational raving, this last plea

at least made sense. The Calabrian operation was in a shambles and all because his mother had mismanaged the land and its workers to the point of revolt and sabotage, something unheard of in his father's time. Now, her pride in taking over where her late husband had left off was on the line—and heaven knew, when it came to pride, Elvira's was unequaled. The Constantino name had been revered in Calabria for centuries; she'd walk over burning coals before she'd allow herself to go down in history as the one who brought dishonor to it.

"I've stated my terms, Elvira," he said, torn between pity and anger. "Treat my wife with respect, and I'll do what I can to put things right on the labor front."

"But of course I will," she almost moaned, pressing her fingertips to her temple and squeezing her eyes closed as if to ward off a clamor of voices only she could hear. "She will become my beloved daughter-in-law."

Really? We'll see, he thought grimly, continuing up the two flights of stairs to the third floor and letting himself into the suite. According to Bianca, their mother's mood swings were becoming both more unpredictable and more extreme, which made her sudden acquiescence to his demands highly suspect.

He found Cassandra taking a nap. She lay on her side on the bed, with one hand tucked beneath her ear, and her legs drawn up as if she were cold. He hadn't dared respond to her touch last night, for fear of where it would have led him. Hadn't dared so much as look at her. But now, with her magical hands and tongue at rest and therefore unable to drive him over the edge, he allowed himself the luxury of examining her, inch by inch, and imagining how it would be, when the danger of her miscarrying was past.

In sleep, her face appeared almost childlike and very

vulnerable. Her mouth was soft and innocent; her brow smooth and untroubled. Carefully, he bent down to sweep a strand of hair from her cheek, and marveled at the texture of both. Silky and golden, just like the soft northern California sunshine of her homeland.

As for her body…his gaze slipped lower, to the even rise and fall of her breasts beneath the loose-fitting top, the sweet curve of her hips and elegant length of leg. Ah, the body was that of a woman, ripe with early pregnancy!

He had never seen her fully naked—not even on the night they'd conceived their child—but the lush contours her clothes couldn't hide offered a tempting preview of all he'd so far missed, and his mouth went dry.

He wanted her. Badly. So much that he was hard and aching, just from looking at her. He wanted to kiss her, touch her, taste her, until her eyes were glazed with passion, and she entreated him, in breathless little sighs, to join his body with hers, and put an end to the madness he'd invoked in her.

He wanted all that and more; had from the second he first set eyes on her. No point in asking himself what it was that made her different from other women he'd known. She simply *was,* that's all, and if he were less the hardheaded businessman and more given to self-delusion, he'd have said that fate, and not Nuncio Zanetti, had had a hand in bringing them together.

She stirred and made a little murmur. Stretched her legs and turned onto her back. Braided her hands over her belly where his child lay sleeping.

Would the baby be a girl who'd grow up beautiful, like her mother? Or a boy, tall like his father, and her willing slave from the moment he took his first breath?

Would there be other babies, conceived at leisure and with love?

As if the intensity of his stare penetrated her sleep, her lashes fluttered, then lifted to reveal fading dreams in her deep blue eyes. Slowly, she rolled her head from side to side, taking in the bedroom's dark, brooding furniture, and as the real world swam back into focus, her brow furrowed and the restful innocence of sleep fled, chased away by an almost fearful uncertainty.

"How long have you been standing here?" she asked in a husky voice.

Gently, he stroked the back of his hand down her cheek. "But a moment or two only, *cara*," he assured her, again questioning his decision to bring her to the palazzo. Coping with a high-risk pregnancy was enough; she didn't need the added burden of dealing with a mother he was beginning to fear was edging disturbingly close to madness.

Cassandra ran her tongue over her lips and swept another glance around the room, this time noticing the shadows of early dusk clouding the tall windows. "What time is it?"

"Almost six o'clock."

"That late? Why didn't you wake me sooner? I was supposed to freshen up and meet you downstairs almost an hour ago!" She sat up and swung her legs over the side of the bed. "I bet your mother's fit to be tied."

"Not at all," he said, steadying her when she lurched to her feet too quickly and swayed dizzily against him. Her skin, where it had been pressed against the pillow, wore the soft, faintly crinkled blush of a newly opened rose, she smelled of warm, lightly perfumed sleep, and it was all he could do not to kiss her. "My mother will understand."

Cassandra flung him an incredulous stare. "Your mother understands nothing about me," she said, pushing him away and clinging to the edge of the bed for support. "I'm an affront to everything she holds dear. She made up her mind to hate me before she ever laid eyes on me."

Turning his mind away from temptation, he took refuge in platitudes which rang hollow even to his ears. "She's set in her ways, that's all. She never expected I'd marry an American, but that's not to say she has anything against you personally."

"Save your breath, Benedict," Cassandra scoffed. "I saw the expression on her face when you introduced us. If it were up to her, she'd have the ground open and swallow me whole."

"But it isn't up to her," he said soothingly, "nor does she make my decisions for me. I married you of my own free will, Cassandra, and while I admit the suddenness of our wedding came as something of a shock to her, now that she's had time to get used to the idea, I think you'll find her more hospitable." He pushed her toward the bathroom. "Take a few minutes to splash some water on your face before we join her in the *salone*. Then you'll see for yourself that what I'm telling you isn't just wishful thinking on my part."

Dubiously, she inspected her sleep-wrinkled clothing and grimaced. "Do you dress for dinner here?"

"As a rule, yes."

"Then it'll take me more than a few minutes to get ready. I'm not showing up looking like a dog's breakfast, and giving her one more reason to despise me."

Given Elvira's often-extraordinary reactions to perfectly ordinary events of late, he couldn't very well argue the point. "Take as long as you like. This is your home away from home, Cassandra. And if my mother has a problem with that, I'll deal with it—and her.''

She looked troubled. "I'm already causing discord between you and her, Benedict. I don't want to create more."

"The discord," he told her, "started long before you entered the picture, *cara*. These days, it seems my mother can't get along with anyone." He gave her a gentle push toward the bathroom. "Go. Do what you have to."

She ran her fingers over her hair. "Is the luggage here yet?"

"*Si*. I brought it up myself. It's in the other room."

"Would you mind going through my suitcase and picking an outfit that you think will serve, while I run a bath?"

"Of course. One of your long skirts and a pretty top will be perfectly acceptable."

She smiled, and he thought that he'd give a very great deal to see her do so more often. "Thank you, Benedict."

"For what? Helping my wife unpack?"

"That, and for being so understanding." She paused in the bathroom doorway. "I'll be quick."

"There's not great rush, *cara*," he said, concerned lest she slip and hurt herself as she climbed in and out of the deep bathtub.

He wished he could stay there to help her; to scrub her back and, when she was all flushed and relaxed, and sweet-smelling from head to toe, to wrap her in a bath sheet. He wished they could bathe together, with her spine resting against his chest and his arms around her. That he could cradle her breasts, slide his hand possessively over the faint swell of her belly, touch her between her legs and make her gasp with pleasure—!

"Benedict," she said, regarding him curiously, "is there something wrong?"

Hell, yes, there was something wrong! He was in acute pain. Again!

"Not a thing, *cara*," he said smoothly. "Enjoy your bath. We usually spend an hour over antipasto and wine before the main meal anyway, but because my mother and I spent longer than planned discussing business, even she won't be her usual punctual self tonight." He checked his watch. "I'll lay out your clothes on the bed and come back for you in, say, half an hour?"

"Come back?" An expression of alarm chased over her face. "Why? Where are you going?"

"I'll shower in my old bachelor suite." *And it will, of necessity, be a very cold shower! Again!* "You'll have the bathroom here all to yourself."

"You know," she said, another her smile dimpling her cheeks bewitchingly, "if you keep spoiling me like this, I'm going to wind up being very glad I married you."

Deciding he'd better put some distance between them before rampant hormones got the better of him, he said with mock severity, "Save the flattery for another occasion, Cassandra, and hop in the tub. We're wasting time."

Oblivious to his discomfort, she flung him a last impish smile, and disappeared into the bathroom.

Elvira Constantino, splendid in a straight black, ankle-length gown whose severity was relieved only by a heavy gold cross and chain, was not alone when Benedict ushered Cassie into the ornate *salone*. A younger woman waited with Elvira, one so closely resembling Benedict and Bianca that Cassie guessed she must be the younger sister, Francesca.

"Well," his mother remarked, coming forward and pressing another of her frigid kisses to Cassie's cheek. "Here you are at last."

"Yes. I'm sorry if we've kept you waiting," Cassie said. "I'm afraid I fell asleep."

"No need to apologize. You've endured an arduous few days, traveling halfway around the world to meet us." The words clinked out of Elvira's mouth as hard as little round pebbles hitting granite, "A siesta is acceptable, under the circumstances."

Sure it is! Cassie thought, containing a shiver. *About as acceptable as if I'd brought the bubonic plague into your house!*

Benedict slipped an arm around her waist and steered her toward the other woman. "Come and meet the baby of the family, *cara*. Francesca, this is my wife, Cassandra. I expect you to take her under your wing and make her feel at home here."

Francesca glanced nervously at her mother, as if requesting direction on how to respond. Elvira replied for her. "Francesca is as busy as you'll be, Benedict. I'm afraid your little bride will have to learn to fend for herself."

"In that case, I'll have to beg off some of the chores you've laid out for me, Mother, and devote my attention to my wife, because I certainly don't intend for her to be neglected."

Although he spoke amicably enough, there was in his tone an undercurrent of steel which persuaded Elvira to take a softer approach. "Of course not, my son. We will all see to it that she is properly entertained."

"I'm perfectly capable of looking out for myself,'' Cassie said, tired of being batted back and forth like a ball between Benedict and his mother. "I've known from the start that this is a working honeymoon for my husband, and certainly don't expect anyone to baby-sit me while he's taking care of business.'' Then, since Francesca still seemed uncertain of how she was supposed to behave, Cassie took her hand and, with a smile, put to use the little bit of Italian she'd practiced earlier. *"Lieto di conoscerla, Francesca!"*

Francesca smiled with delight, but Elvira let out a squawk of unkind laughter. "As you said, Benedict, your wife does not speak Italian!''

Cassie heard the hiss of his indrawn breath, saw the angry throbbing of the pulse at his temple, and knew he'd have leaped to her defense again, had she not beaten him to it. "But I'm willing to try,'' she said, fixing her mother-in-law in a forthright stare. "Shouldn't that count for something?''

For a moment, Elvira stared right back, the contempt in her eyes so apparent that a person would have had to be blind to miss it. Then she dropped her gaze and said, *"Si.* Of course. It counts.'' She waved her garnet-tipped fingers to the windows at the far end of the room. "Francesca, show our guest the view, and I will ring for Speranza to bring in the antipasto and wine.''

"I'm very happy to meet you,'' Francesca whispered, leading Cassie to a quartet of chairs facing a breathtaking panorama of sea and sky painted in varying shades of purple now that the sun had slipped below the horizon. "And please, Cassandra, do not take to heart the things my mother sometimes says. Calabrian women are very possessive of their sons, you see, and she had other hopes for Benedict.''

Before Cassie could ask what they were, the door opened and she received her answer as another young woman entered the room. Cooing as sweetly as a dove, even if she looked more like a marauding crow, Elvira swooped over and enfolded her in a warm embrace.

"Her name is Giovanna," Francesca murmured, under cover of the ensuing babble of conversation.

"And she's the 'other hope'?"

"*Si*. I'm afraid so."

"Is she in love with Benedict?" Cassie asked, watching as the woman turned to greet him continental style, with a kiss on both cheeks.

"I think most unmarried women in Calabria are a little in love with Benedict," Francesca said with a laugh, "and some of the married ones, as well, if truth be told. But Giovanna will not try to encroach on your relationship with him. She is a good woman."

She was a very pretty woman, too, with a sweet face and gently voluptuous body, and her smile, as she came to where Cassie and Francesca sat, seemed sincere. "You are Benedict's Cassandra, and I am Giovanna," she said, her English even more polished than Elvira's. "It is a pleasure to welcome you to Calabria."

She sat in the chair next to Cassie's and asked about the flight over, how she'd liked the little she'd seen of Milan, and what she thought of Italy so far. "If you'd like a tour guide while you're in Calabria, please call on me," she said. "I'd be honored to show you the sights."

Francesca was right, Cassie soon realized. This woman posed no threat to the marriage. The danger came from the mother, and feeling Elvira's inimical gaze on her, Cassie drew her silk shawl more snugly around her shoulders.

After a few minutes, Speranza shuffled into the room,

pushing a carved wooden trolley bearing a carafe of wine, and a heavy platter containing a selection of smoked fish, olives, marinated vegetables, and tiny rounds of sausage.

"All local specialties," Francesca explained. "In fact, the olives come from our own land."

And no doubt they were all delicious. But the spicy smell of the sausage and the sight of the pimento-stuffed olives glistening under a light coat of oil, left Cassie fighting a sudden wave of nausea.

Noticing what she perceived to be her guest's distaste, Elvira inquired archly, "You do not care for our food, Cassandra?"

"Not right now," she managed to say, dabbing at the perspiration dotting her forehead.

Benedict, bless his heart, realized her distress and came forward with a glass of sparkling water to which he'd added a sliver of lime. "Here, *cara,*" he said quietly. "Sip this. It will help."

Elvira's sharp gaze missed not a thing. "You do not care for our wine, either? What a shame!"

"It's not your wine in particular," Cassie replied. "It's any sort of wine."

"Ah, *cara,* you have a problem with alcohol!" Elvira could barely contain her glee at uncovering what she deemed to be yet another fatal flaw in the woman her son had claimed for a wife.

"I'm not a recovering addict, if that's what you're implying," Cassie said, rallying to her own defense. "I'm just avoiding all alcohol right now, and I'd have thought you'd understand the reason for it."

"How is that possible?" Elvira tilted one shoulder in a dismissive shrug. "You are a stranger to me. Until a few days ago, I knew nothing of your existence. How can I be expected to know the reason behind your likes and dislikes, unless you explain them to me?''

"Stop pressuring her, Mother! Cassandra said 'no' to wine. Be content with that, and find something else to talk about!''

The speed with which he intervened on her behalf, not to mention the sharpness with which he uttered his rebuke, would have warmed Cassie's heart, had it not been for her sudden suspicion that Benedict had been very selective in what he'd told his mother. Unless Cassie was totally misreading the situation, Elvira might have been informed of her son's marriage, but she hadn't a clue his bride was pregnant.

Even more startling, though, was the effect his words had on his mother. Thoroughly subdued, she sank into the nearest chair, and when she spoke again, her intonation flowed like music, instead of snapping with malice. "I hope your suite of rooms is to your liking, child. The third floor isn't used very much anymore, but I thought that, as a new bride, you would enjoy the privacy it affords.''

"That's…very considerate of you,'' Cassie said, taken aback by the sudden about-face.

"But how else should I be? You are *la mia nuora*— how do you say in English? My daughter-by-law?''

"Daughter-in-law,'' Francesca supplied.

"Just so.'' Elvira sipped her wine and subjected Cassie to such a long scrutiny that Cassie began to squirm "It's a big adjustment, coming to a country where you don't speak the language or understand local customs,'' she finally decreed. "And then, there is the fact that we're almost nine hours ahead of California time. You've come a long way to meet us, and I can see that it's left you very weary. I should have arranged for you to eat a light supper in your suite and make an early night of it.''

Deciding this was as good a time as any to mention her pregnancy, Cassie began, ''Well, it's not just the travel or jet lag that's wiping me out. It's—''

But Benedict, catching her eye and realizing her intent, gave the merest shake of his head. ''It was all the running around she had to do before she left San Francisco that's left her so exhausted,'' he cut in deftly. ''Cassandra runs a very successful business and had to make sure it would operate smoothly during her absence.''

If steering the conversation into a different channel had been his intent, he succeeded. Throughout the remainder of the cocktail hour, Cassie was peppered with questions from Francesca and Giovanna, who wanted to know everything about her life in California.

Dusk was well on its way to night before the evening meal was served in a dining hall resembling something out of the sixteenth century, with massive furniture elaborately carved like that in the *salone,* and rich velvet tapestries on the walls. Easily capable of seating twenty, the table was set with engraved sterling and cut crystal so heavy, it could have knocked a grown man senseless. Taking her assigned place, Cassie thought the only thing missing were ladies in period costume and a troubadour playing a mandolin in the minstrel's gallery.

Conversation was lively enough, although Elvira, for the most part, leaned back in her chair and appeared totally oblivious to her surroundings. Once or twice, her glance fell on Cassie and lingered there, and if her brief show of kindness was gone, so was her hostility. If anything, she looked puzzled, as if she couldn't recall the reason this stranger was at her table. Finally, just before coffee was served, she abruptly got up from her chair and, without a word of explanation, wandered to the door.

Obviously irritated, Benedict said, "Where are you going, Mother?"

"To bed," she said, pressing a hand to her temple. "I have a headache and need to lie down."

"She's complained often of headaches in the last little while," Francesca explained, after the door had closed behind her mother. "Usually, they're preceded by a terrible burst of temper over something quite trivial."

"Has she seen a doctor?" he asked.

"No, although I've suggested it more than once. But she claims stress is the cause, and Benedict, we all know she's got plenty of that. The situation here goes from bad to worse on a daily basis."

"Bianca already filled me in," he said, flinging her a quelling glance, "but Cassandra doesn't need to burdened with the details."

"I don't see why not, if I'm now part of the family," Cassie said.

"Because you have enough to deal with, *cara.* Bad enough that my mother's feeling the strain, without it infecting you, too."

"But perhaps I can help."

"No." Not for a second did he consider the possibility.

"Please stop treating me as I'm made of glass, Benedict," she said, covering up her annoyance with a laugh. "You said yourself, I'm an experienced businesswoman, so don't be so ready to dismiss my offer to help, either—at least not without giving me a reason."

"You're my wife," he said brusquely. "And as your

husband, I'm saying I don't want you involved. That's reason enough.''

Her mouth fell open in shock, and it took her a moment to recover enough to say, ''I *beg* your pardon?''

''This is not America, Cassandra,'' he declared. ''Here, a wife knows her place—''

''*Knows her place?*'' She stared at him, unable to believe her ears or his arrogance.

''Exactly,'' he said calmly. ''And it is not necessarily at her husband's side where business is concerned.''

''Really? What a pity you didn't choose to tell me before we were married that your idea of how to treat a wife is keeping her barefoot, pregnant, and tied to the kitchen sink. If you had, I can assure you, it would have made all the difference in the world to how I'd have received your proposal.''

''It's a little late in the day for that, wouldn't you say?''

''Trust me, Benedict, it's never too late!''

Giovanna cleared her throat and muttered, ''Come, Francesca, let's take our coffee in the *salone*.''

Cassie shoved back her chair and flung down her napkin. ''No need,'' she fumed, so furious she could have choked Benedict on the spot. ''I'm more than happy to be the one to leave.''

''But you're on your honeymoon…!'' Distressed, Francesca appealed to her brother. ''Benedict, please say something!''

''It's okay, Francesca,'' Cassie said. ''He's said enough and frankly, I've had about as much of the Constantino brand of hospitality as I can stomach for one day! The lord and master's all yours, ladies, and I wish you both the joy of him!''

CHAPTER EIGHT

HE SHOWED up in the suite some fifteen minutes later. By then, she'd changed and was buttoned up to the throat in the longest, most concealing nightgown she'd brought with her, and sat at the old-fashioned dressing table, furiously brushing her hair.

"We need to talk," he announced, coming up behind her and attempting to take the brush from her hand. "I realize you found my manner downstairs to be somewhat abrupt—"

She yanked the brush out of his reach and briefly debated swatting him with it. *"Abrupt?"* she repeated, trying very hard not to screech with the rage consuming her. "Try 'overbearing, high-handed, rude and obnoxious' on for size. I think you'll find any, or all descriptions, will fit!"

He looked pained. "You know, Cassandra," he said, "you're not the only one who's had enough grief for one day. I'm about at the end of my rope, too, and in no mood to deal with yet another temperamental woman. That being so, please shut up long enough to hear me out. Then, if you still feel like raking your nails down my face—"

"Hardly!" she scoffed. "That might be the only way the women around here can vent their frustration when it comes to dealing with deranged chauvinists, but where I come from, we choose more sophisticated methods of getting even."

"I can hardly wait to experience them firsthand," he

said drily. "In the meantime, however, allow me clarify what I started to say before you left the dining room."

"I didn't *leave* the dining room, Benedict," she informed him waspishly. "I stormed out in high dudgeon, and if you were one-tenth as perceptive as you like to think you are, you'd recognize how thoroughly ticked off I had to be, to do that in front of people I've only just met, and you'd modify your attitude accordingly—always assuming, of course, that you're the least bit interested in keeping me around as your wife."

"Don't threaten me, Cassandra," he warned her. "We are married and will remain so, at least as long as you're carrying my child."

Refusing to acknowledge the sliver of unease *that* revealing little slip of the tongue produced, she said rashly, "And after that, do you plan to ship me off to a nunnery?"

He shrugged. "Maybe even *before* then, if I deem it necessary."

"Well, at least that would spare you having to explain to your mother that I'm pregnant, wouldn't it? Why so reluctant to spread the good news, Benedict? Could it be that you're ashamed to have her know you're not quite as perfect as she'd like to believe?"

"I'm protecting you, Cassandra. There'll be time enough to broadcast word of the baby once my mother's become reconciled to the fact of our marriage. You're too intelligent not to have noticed that she's hardly overjoyed by it, and I see no point in exacerbating an already delicate situation, particularly not if you're the one who'll bear the brunt of it."

"Why just me? Conceiving our child was a joint endeavor, in case you've forgotten."

"I've forgotten nothing," he said sharply, "nor do I

wish to become further embroiled in argument with you, so kindly be still and pay attention to what I'm about to tell you.''

Oh! *Ohh!* Seething, she said, ''Stop treating me as if I'm some medieval...*wench!*''

That stopped him short! ''I don't know this word, 'wench.' What does it mean?''

''An inferior female designed for your pleasure, however you choose to take it.''

''What a novel concept,'' he remarked thoughtfully. ''I shall keep it in mind for future reference. For now, however, I prefer to focus on the immediate present, which brings me back to what I was trying to explain, before you went flying off at a tangent.''

She'd have repudiated that allegation, too, if she'd had the chance, but he steamrolled right over her and launched into part two of his lecture. ''This is not San Francisco, Cassandra. It isn't even *Roma* or *Milano* or *Firenze*. It is a small, ancient part of Italy with customs which go back centuries and which, in many respects, lags decades behind the rest of the country in its attitudes and outlook. Calabrian women do not, as a rule, enjoy the kind of professional prominence their counterparts in America take for granted—particularly not in family-run enterprises like ours, with international connections. They stick instead to more traditional roles.''

''Really?'' She flung him a blistering glare through the warped glass of the mirror. ''I guess someone forgot to tell your mother that.''

''My mother wasn't active in any of our business dealings until she became widowed. Had there been another son, or if Francesca had a husband, *he* would have been the one to take over where my father left off. But there was neither, and because she's more familiar with the local end of our industry than anyone else in the area, my mother tried to step into my father's shoes.''

''Which you find perfectly acceptable, as long as your wife doesn't—''

''I found it acceptable at first, because our workers had been with us for generations and were very loyal to our family name,'' he said, drowning her out in a tone of voice she was quickly learning to hate. ''With their cooperation, I had every reason to believe the operation here would continue to run smoothly.''

''But Mother's taken on more than she can handle, right?''

Before answering, he hesitated just long enough to make her suspect he was choosing his next words with extreme care. Not lying, exactly, but *laundering* the truth. ''It would appear so. Over the last several months, our most prized product, the bergamot, has not yielded as expected. Even more disturbing, our orchards and olive groves have been severely vandalized, thereby endangering next year's crops. I surely don't need to spell out for you the ramifications of such action.''

That he was worried was apparent, and she could understand why. ''No, you don't,'' she said. ''Wilful destruction of property is a serious matter on more than just a monetary front. It speaks of criminal intent and poses a very real danger to anyone attempting to put an end to it.''

''Precisely. I'm not anxious for my own safety, Cassandra, but for yours, and that's why I don't want you assuming any sort of public profile while we're here. The less attention drawn to you, the better I'll like it.''

Her annoyance softening under the warmth of his obvious concern, she said, ''Do you know who's responsible for the vandalism?''

"I suspect it's retaliation from certain unscrupulous and dissatisfied employees."

"What do you propose to do about it?"

"Reestablish the old order of things." He glanced at her almost apologetically. "It might mean extending our time here."

A horrifying thought struck her. "You're not hinting at relocating here permanently and taking your mother's place, are you?" she asked with unvarnished dismay.

"No," he said, firmly enough to reassure her. "You know how, as a family, we've divided responsibility among us. My place is not here at the local level. But if production of our fundamental resources cannot be implemented, we'll all be looking for other ways to make a living."

"My goodness, I had no idea things were as bad as this." She chewed her lip thoughtfully. "If cash flow's a problem, I might be able to help. No one but you and I would need to know."

"Not as long as I have breath in my body, Cassandra! I no more married you for your money, than you married me for mine."

"Well, of course you didn't, because you didn't know exactly how much I'm worth, but it just so happens that my grandmother left me a sizable inheritance."

"I don't care if she left you the Hope Diamond," he said flatly. "This is not your problem, and I won't have you involved in trying to resolve it."

"So who *will* you call on, then? The police?"

"No." He picked up her brush and began stroking it through her hair. "We are a small community. Everyone here is related, either directly or through marriage, to his neighbor. Even if it were possible to identify those responsible for causing the damage, we'd gain nothing but ill will by pressing formal charges. A man behind bars cannot provide for his family, and family in this part of the world is paramount. Punish one member, and you punish them all.''

Appalled, she said, "So you're letting felons go free? That doesn't make much sense! You're just encouraging more trouble."

"The Constantinos have a reputation to uphold, and they do it with their own brand of justice, not one imposed by the state. Until this recent crisis, our employees have known they could depend on us to treat them fairly and with respect. I must prove to them that such a tradition has not been abandoned."

"What makes you think they'll believe you?"

"I grew up here. I understand the people and they understand me. In the past, we have enjoyed a mutual trust, and my first task is to reestablish it. Once that is done, I'll deal with anyone still inclined toward inflicting damage to our property."

"I don't much like the sound of that! What about the risks you'd be taking?"

"They'd be no worse than facing your wrath, *cara*," he said lightly.

Too lightly! He might be unspeakably bossy and annoying on occasion, but he was her husband and she realized that, in a remarkably short space of time, she'd grown very fond of the idea. The thought of him putting himself in the line of fire filled her with dismay.

Wishing she hadn't been so quick to lose her temper with him, she said, "You should have told me all this sooner."

"I'd have preferred never to have mentioned it at all." He returned the hairbrush to the dressing table and rested his hands on her shoulders. "Our honeymoon's facing enough hurdles, without burdening it further with my problems.''

She leaned back and rested against him, loving the sense of security it gave her. Small wonder his field hands trusted him. He exuded a strength and integrity that inspired confidence, and made anything seem possible.

''Sharing problems is what being married's all about, Benedict,'' she murmured, closing her eyes.

For the space of a minute or two, he massaged her shoulders gently. And then, almost imperceptibly, his fingers slid to the base of her throat and grew still. ''It's about more than that, *cara mia*,'' he said hoarsely.

She heard the tortured desire behind his words, and her blood raced. ''I know,'' she said, and drew his hand down to her breast.

It remained there, shaping her so possessively, so sensuously, that her flesh ached and a bolt of sensation shot the length of her, to settle between her legs.

With a soft gasp of pleasure, she opened her eyes and looked in the mirror. She saw his gaze fixed on her reflection, mesmerized by her rapid breathing, the heightened color in her cheeks, the wild flutter of the pulse below her jaw. She saw the dark fire in his eyes and knew that hers was not the only heart leaping to win a race it had already lost.

Her glance dropped. As she watched, his hands inched deliberately to the buttons at her throat, undid them, and pushed the nightgown over her shoulders and down her arms, until it fell to her waist. And all the time, he stared at her in the mirror, gauging her response, knowing he was driving her mad.

''Don't stop, Benedict!'' she begged, on a broken sigh.

In answer, he lowered his head to kiss the side of her neck, then whispered in her ear, and she didn't need to understand Italian to know that he was speaking the language of love—of making love—in very explicit terms.

He leaned farther over her and she, cradled against his hips, reveled in the urgent thrust of his arousal between her shoulder blades. His lips trailed over the upper slope of one breast, delineating the blue veins marking her skin, before his mouth found her nipple and tugged at it gently.

Saliva pooled under her tongue, and a tiny cry escaped her. She squirmed on the padded bench. Felt the heat tracing arcs of lightning at her core.

She tried to turn but he held her imprisoned against his erection, pushed her nightgown lower, and spread his palms over her belly.

"Benedict...!" she implored, and reaching behind, slid her hands up the back of his spread thighs to their apex, and caressed the masculine configuration clustered there.

This time, he was the one who groaned, a feral, primitive sound. The sound of a warrior facing insurmountable odds.

He lifted his head again to look at her. His eyes smoldered like embers, and his chest heaved. But tonight he was not a man to submit to her wiles, no matter how powerful they might be. Instead, he fought back.

He pushed her gown lower and slipped his hand between her legs. No more able to resist his invasion than any other part of her, they fell slackly apart and gave him access. He delved deep between the moist, silken folds of her flesh and found the spot quivering at her center.

He touched it. Just once.

It was enough.

She convulsed.

Prisms of color swirled through her mind, suffused her senses. Hot, blinding. Her body clenched, released. Clenched again. And again and again, until she thought she'd faint from the sublime torture of it.

But he was horrified at what he'd effected. Withdrawing his hand, he wrapped his arms around her and held her tight, as if afraid she might fly apart if he didn't contain her.

"Don't worry, Benedict," she whispered, sensing his fear and wanting to reassure him. Wanting, if truth be told, for more—for him to lose himself inside her. "I'm fine."

"No," he said, his face a mask of misery. "I had no right to do that."

"You had every right," she breathed, reaching up to touch his cheek. "I'm your wife. What just happened between us is perfectly natural."

"No," he said again, releasing her and stepping safely out of temptation's way. "It was unwise. You could miscarry—"

"I'm not going to miscarry. We're going to have a healthy baby."

Unconvinced, he paced about the room. "Do you feel...anything?"

She'd have smiled at the question, except she knew that he was in no mood for levity. "I feel cherished."

"No cramping or discomfort?"

"Just the ache of fulfillment, and I think that's allowed."

"I didn't marry you for sex," he reminded her grimly. "I married you because you're expecting my child. If, because of something I've done, you should lose the baby…''

"What?" she said, a bleak chill replacing the warm and lovely sensations of a moment ago. "You'd apply for an annulment the very next day?"

"I'd never forgive myself."

"Well, Benedict," she said, pulling her nightgown back where it belonged and doing up the buttons, "I have a feeling it's really not in your hands. Nature has a way of taking care of itself where pregnancy's concerned. Just because we have to be careful for the next little while doesn't mean you have to behave as if I'm made of porcelain, liable to shatter at the slightest touch."

"I'm not prepared to take the chance. There'll be no more incidents like this, Cassandra, until your doctor gives the word."

There might just as well never have been an incident like that to begin with! The passion he'd barely been able to hold in check had metamorphosed into a reserve so cool that it reminded her of the sea fog, slinking up from San Francisco Bay to leave its clammy imprint on every room in her town house.

Depressed, she pushed back the bench and went into the bathroom. She was willing to give him everything of herself, and she wanted the same from him. But he was determined to allow her only a little, and while it was, in itself, overwhelming and magnificent, it wasn't enough.

Was she asking too much, she wondered, as she brushed her teeth. Was the outpouring of emotional generosity she felt, simply a woman thing, which men didn't understand and couldn't emulate?

She had no answers, nor was he forthcoming with any

because, when she returned to the bedroom, it was to find him gone. Her one consolation at being once more abandoned for the night was the realization that, however much it might irk him, he knew the only way he could keep a lid on the sexual attraction sizzling between them, was for him to stay away from her.

They were just finishing a breakfast of fruit, sweet rolls and coffee the next morning, when Cassie mentioned her intention to walk into the village to do some shopping. With the threat of so much idle time on her hands, she wanted to start making items for the baby's layette, but needed to buy supplies.

"No," Benedict said.

"What do you mean, *no?*" Taken aback by his instant and adamant veto, she stared at him indignantly.

"I mean, absolutely not," he said. "In fact, I forbid it."

Was this the same man who, with a single touch, had reduced her to incoherent ecstasy last night? Who, for a few stolen moments, had shown such a caring side to his nature that she'd all but fallen in love with him?

"Benedict," she said, articulating each word slowly and distinctly, just to make sure he received the message she was determined to convey, "first of all, I won't allow you to forbid me to do anything. And second, there's nothing here to keep me occupied."

Nor was there, unless rattling around in the gloomy old palazzo was considered entertainment. Francesca and Elvira had left a few minutes before for the office, to do whatever it was they did there—the latter again bestowing a puzzled glance at Cassie as if she hadn't the foggiest idea who she was—and Benedict was about to go off for a meeting with those men still willing to work the estate.

"It's too far for you to walk to the village," he said, not sparing her even a glance, so busy was he perusing a computer printout. "And even if it weren't, I doubt you'd find what you're looking for there."

"Then I'll take your car and drive to the nearest town."

"No."

Doing her best to hang on to her temper, she said curtly, "Are you afraid I might dent its precious fender? Get stopped for speeding? Trade it in for a Vespa and go whizzing all over the countryside, leaving a trail of destruction in my wake?"

Oblivious to her mounting irritation, he calmly flipped over a page, and took a mouthful of coffee before saying, yet again, "No."

"Damn it, Benedict!" Totally out of patience, she slammed her hand down on the table hard enough to make him look up. "Is that your answer for everything this morning?"

"If you want to go shopping, Cassandra," he said mildly, "I will take you, as soon as I can spare the time."

"I don't need to be *taken* anywhere," she snapped, surreptitiously stroking her other hand over her stinging palm. "I'm perfectly capable of following a map and I have an international driver's license, so what's your real objection?"

"I don't want you wandering around by yourself outside the palazzo."

"Why ever not?"

"I thought I explained my reasons, last night."

"On the workfront, yes, you did, but this goes beyond

that. For heaven's sake, on the street among other people, I could pass for just another tourist.''

''It's too early in the season for tourists, and you're too blond and foreign-looking to pass unnoticed, even in a crowd.''

''But—!''

Exasperated, he slapped the computer sheets on the table. ''But nothing! The plain fact of the matter is, I'm concerned for your safety, Cassandra. I don't want you to become the target of…mischief.''

''What kind of mischief? You think a disgruntled former employee might make off with me?''

''Yes,'' he said levelly. ''That's exactly what I'm afraid might happen.''

Swallowing the incredulous laugh rising in her throat, because there was no mistaking how utterly serious he was, she said, ''You think I could be *kidnapped?*''

''It's a distinct possibility, and a risk I'm not willing to take.''

''So I'm to stay cooped up inside this place?''

''If you find the idea so distasteful, there are acres of walled garden for you to enjoy, and a private beach, inaccessible to outsiders, where you can swim or sunbathe.'' He drained his cup, set it down with a decisive clink, and rose from his chair. ''I have to go. Please, Cassandra, don't defy me on this. Stay within the palazzo grounds. I've got enough on my mind, without having to worry about you.''

''Is worrying about my being held for ransom the reason you decided not to sleep in our suite last night?'' she said bitterly.

He stopped on his way to the door, and flung her a hunted look. ''Your safety here is not an issue. The pal-

azzo is secure. And you know very well why I didn't
sleep with you last night.''

In truth, he didn't look as if he'd slept at all. Grooves
of weariness bracketed his mouth, and she felt suddenly
ashamed for plaguing him, when he clearly had very
pressing matters weighing on his mind.

Contrite, she said, ''Yes, I do know why. But I wish
you'd reconsider, Benedict. We might not be able to
make love, but if we could at least spend the nights
together, I'd find it much easier to accept your not being
with me during the day.''

''Sleeping beside his wife, knowing he can't make
love to her, demands superhuman control of a man, and
I'm far from sure I'm up to the challenge. But if it's that
important to you, we can give it a try. Meanwhile, please
accept that I'm not trying to come across as the heavy-
handed husband, just to make you miserable.''

''I realize that. I can see that you're concerned.''

He brushed a kiss over her mouth. ''Then please, for
your own sake, stay put here until I'm free to escort you
elsewhere. All other considerations apart, you saw for
yourself, yesterday, how brutal the roads are around
here.''

''Oh, yes!'' She gave a shudder of mock horror. ''I
was white-knuckled with nerves every time you stepped
on the gas. And I almost had a heart attack when we
rounded that one corner, and came nose to nose with a
donkey pulling a cart and leaving no room for us to
pass.''

''Which is why I can't see you being comfortable
driving an unfamiliar car in such unforgiving, unfamiliar
territory. Trust me on this, Cassandra. I really do have
your best interests at heart.''

She tucked her hand under his arm and walked with

him to the door. That morning, he wore jeans, a white T-shirt, and sturdy work boots, yet even in such casual garb, he still managed to look like royalty. "I do trust you," she said softly. "And you can trust me. I won't stray from the property, Benedict, I promise."

"Thank you!" For a moment, she thought he was going to kiss her again. His hands came up to frame her face. Then, at the last moment, he backed away. "I'll see you tonight at dinner."

"Not before? What about lunch?"

"I'll eat with the field hands. But if I'm able to get enough accomplished in the next couple of days, we'll spend the weekend at my summer place in Sicily."

It didn't happen. Not only was the Sicilian trip put on hold, but their supposed two-week stay drifted into three, then four. Knowing from the comments he let slip, that a mountain of work still lay ahead before the orchards and groves were restored to full operating capacity, Cassie refrained from pestering him any more than she could help, about when they'd be going back to the US.

For his part, to relieve the tedium and give her something to occupy the long hours she spent alone, Benedict arranged for Bianca to mail her a layette package containing sewing and knitting supplies, with patterns for little jackets and hats, and directions for making a lovely hand-quilted crib cover. Cassie had to work on them in secret, of course, so as not to give away the fact of her pregnancy, but at least they gave her a sense of purpose.

They also saved her sanity, because in the days after that, she saw so little of Benedict that she began to wonder if he was deliberately avoiding her. Those times they were together, he was so preoccupied and distant that although he'd given in to her request that they sleep together, she felt no real sense of connection between them.

Oh, he provided for her well enough. She had a roof over her head, food on the table, a perfunctory peck on the cheek each night and morning. But a warm body to curl up against at night? She might as well have been lying next to one of his mother's precious marble statues!

It wasn't that she expected him to break their agreement, but did their not making love mean they couldn't show each other normal affection? It appeared so. In many ways, he was now more a stranger than he had been the night she conceived his child.

If Cassie didn't see much of her husband, though, she saw more than enough of Elvira. The minute she stepped out of the suite, the woman emerged from the shadows, a silent, disapproving figure on constant surveillance.

What did she think—that her son's wife might try to steal the family silver? Deface the paintings on the walls? Take her manicure scissors to the tapestries?

To escape the oppressive atmosphere, Cassie spent as much time as possible on the beach. It became her haven, the one place she found peace and a temporary sense of freedom. Down there, out of sight of the house, she could sit in the shade of an umbrella and work on her baby's layette, laze on the pale gold scimitar of sand, or swim in the clear blue sea, without fear of censure.

As April slipped into May, however, the temperature soared and to avoid the worst of the heat, she was forced to spend more time in the palazzo where she took refuge upstairs, on the sitting room balcony overlooking the shadowed courtyard. It was then, hemmed in by the claustrophobic atmosphere, that she missed her own home and her own friends so acutely.

Her occasional phone calls to Trish did help, but the only telephone in the residential part of the palazzo was in the entrance hall. Trying to conduct a private conversation there was near impossible, with Elvira frequently lurking in the background.

"Having fun?" Trish would ask.

"Hardly," Cassie would mutter, peering furtively over her shoulder. "Much more of this, and I'll be crawling around on my hands and knees, barking at the moon."

"Still not getting along with the mother-in-law?"

"Not a chance. Most of the time, she's got the temperament of a pit viper. The rest, she's so spaced out, it's enough to make a person wonder if she's on drugs."

"And she still hasn't clued in to the reason you're wandering around the place wearing tent dresses?"

"Apparently not."

"What about the sister?"

"Oh, Francesca's a darling, and so is Giovanna. If it weren't for the two of them acting as a buffer between me and Elvira, it'd be open war around here. But they're both as caught up in the family business as Benedict, so I don't see much more of them than I do of him."

"Well, hang in there, kiddo! With everyone working around the clock to put things in order, this can't go on much longer. And don't worry about a thing at this end. Although everyone here misses you, we're coping, and business is booming."

Yes—booming without her!

Then, as if all that weren't misery enough, Benedict sought her out one day and said, "I'm going to have to leave you here alone for a few days, Cassandra. There's a matter to be dealt with elsewhere."

Her heart plummeted with fear. She knew immediately, from his somber expression, that the "matter" had to do with meting out to those responsible for the vandalism, the Constantino brand of justice he'd spoken of weeks before.

"I can't do this anymore!" she cried brokenly. "I can't, Benedict! I've had enough. You married me and brought me here, for the baby's sake and because you believe family should come first, yet here I am, growing bigger by the day, and to maintain peace with your benighted mother, I have to keep my pregnancy secret. And now, on top of that, I have to worry that you're going to get yourself killed by a bunch of thugs, because you're too proud to enlist police help?"

"It's the way it has to be," he said, attempting to corral her in his arms.

She fought him off and dashed the angry tears from her eyes. "*No!* I won't do it. I won't wait here for them to bring your broken body back, and be left a widow before I've known what's it like to become a real wife."

He hitched one hip on the edge of the bedroom dresser and, overcoming her resistance, drew her into the vee of his thighs, close enough that she could feel the heat of his body, and smell the residue of sun-baked earth on his skin.

"Don't give up on us now, *cara*," he begged. "Once this last matter is settled, I'll be finished here, and will take you home again. You'll be back with your own kind long before the baby's born, I promise."

"But can you promise that you'll be there, as well?"

"Of course. This is my child, too."

If only he'd said, *Of course, because I love you!* she would have agreed to anything. But what was the point in wishing for the moon when, from the outset, he'd been very clear that love didn't enter the equation?

Pressing her lips together hard to prevent herself from bursting into tears, she said "Let go of me, Benedict."

But he wouldn't release her. "No," he said. "It's been too long since I held you in my arms." His gaze fell to her mouth and remained there. "Too long since I kissed you," he said, and let his own mouth following his glance.

One kiss was all it took. Just that swiftly, that help-lessly, she capitulated. She knew she'd hate them both afterward—him for being such a masterful lover, and herself for being too spineless to resist him—but for now, all that emblazoned itself on her consciousness was easing the desperate hunger which had beset her for so long.

To have him hold her as if she were the most precious creature in the world, to feel his mouth claiming hers with such unrestrained passion, was all that counted. Time enough tomorrow, when he'd have left her again, to dwell on regret and to despise them both.

CHAPTER NINE

HE LEFT the following morning, and for the next three days and nights, she was so consumed with fear for his safety that she thought she'd go mad. Finally, on the afternoon of the fourth day, and unable to stand her own company a moment longer, Cassie picked up her phrase book and made her way to the kitchen in search of Speranza, the one person who, from the very beginning, had always treated her with kindness.

Although equipped with enough modern appliances to make it reasonably efficient, the kitchen bore many reminders of an earlier era. Braids of garlic and dried peppers decorated the walls, an open-fire brick oven filled one corner, and iron pots and pans hung from hooks above the stove. In Cassie's opinion, it was by far the most cheerful room in the house and she wished she'd found it sooner.

Speranza was rolling out dough at a big scrubbed table in the middle of the floor, but she dusted off her hands when she saw she had a visitor.

"La disturbo?" Cassie asked.

"No!" The dear old soul broke into a welcoming smile, and with much effusive gesturing, led her to a rocking chair beside the oven. *"Avanti, e si accomodi, per favore!"*

Wishing she had a better grasp of the language, Cassie flipped through her phrase book, searching for the words to explain her presence, but couldn't find anything appropriate. "I'm afraid I don't speak much Italian—*non parlo italiano.*"

Speranza nodded enthusiastically and waited, her wrinkled face alive with curiosity.

Feeling decidedly foolish, Cassie waved her hands and said, "I came to see you because it's lonely upstairs, all by myself—*sola.*"

"*Sola. Si!*" Another smile, this one full of sympathy.

"I thought we might have coffee together." She touched her fingertips to her heart, then gestured at Speranza. "*Caffe*—you and me?"

"*Non caffe!*" Tutting with disapproval, the old woman bustled to the refrigerator, and took out a pottery jug. "*Latte—per bambino,*" she said, pouring a glass of milk and handing it to Cassie.

Startled, Cassie splayed her hands across her middle. "Benedict told you about the *bambino?*"

Speranza knew enough English to understand the question, but not enough to reply with words. Instead, she shook her head, and tapped her temple with a work-gnarled forefinger.

Taken aback, Cassie exclaimed, "You *guessed?*"

More nodding, and the widest, warmest smile yet.

"Oh…" Overcome with emotion, Cassie fought a rush of tears. "You don't know how good it feels to be able to talk openly about it. No one else knows, you see. Benedict's reluctant to say anything. Perhaps, he's embarrassed." She hunted through her phrase book, and found the word she was looking for. "Benedict *è imbarazzato.*"

Aghast at the suggestion, Speranza held out a peremptory hand for the book and riffled through the vocabulary section at the back. After much concentration, she spoke, and if the pronunciation was a bit garbled, there was no mistaking her meaning. "No, *signora*. Signor Benedict, he is proud."

"I don't know, Speranza." Cassie stroked her hand over her midriff again, then touched her wedding ring. "He only married me because of the *bambino*."

This time, her message went astray, and it was pretty obvious from Speranza's knowing smile that her reply had more to do with Benedict's sperm count than his sense of honor. "*Si*. Signor Benedict *è molto virile!*"

"He's all that and then some," Cassie agreed ruefully. "The trouble is, I can never tell whether he's simply being kind and decent because he got me pregnant, or if he really cares about me, regardless of the baby."

She knew she was she was pouring out her heart to someone who hadn't the faintest idea what she was running on about, but the relief of being able to give voice to feelings she'd kept bottled up for so long felt wonderful. What Speranza made of it all, though, was impossible to tell. She clucked to herself, regarded Cassie thoughtfully when the spate of words came to an end, then took her hand and, turning it over, carefully inspected the palm.

Finally, she pushed the untouched milk closer, flexed the muscles in her skinny, wrinkled arms, and announced, "Is *figlio*. Drink, *signora, per bambino*. For boy baby to be *forte* like Papa."

Whether it was the lively delight in Speranza's dark eyes, or the sight of her surprisingly firm little round biceps that had Cassie bursting into giggles, hardly mattered. It was enough that, for what seemed like the first time in forever, *something* was truly funny.

"Oh, Speranza," she spluttered, almost choking on the milk, "you can't begin to know how good it feels to laugh again!"

But the merriment died as swiftly as it had arisen when a voice, sharp as a knife blade, cut through the cheerful atmosphere to inquire, "So what is it you find so amusing, Cassandra, that you take my servant away from her duties in this fashion?"

Wiping her eyes, Cassie looked over her shoulder. Elvira stood in the doorway, her face livid with controlled rage and her fury-filled breathing stripping every vestige of lightheartedness from the room.

How long had she been hovering there, like a big black vulture come to wreak vengeance on heaven knew what? Had she heard them talking about the baby? And what sort of price was Speranza going to have to pay for fraternizing with the enemy? Because that this was one of those days when Cassie had once again been cast in the role of adversary in her mother-in-law's eyes, was pretty hard to miss.

"Please don't blame Speranza," she blurted out, leaping from the rocking chair so suddenly that her stomach churned. "I came here uninvited, looking for a cup of coffee, and didn't mean to distract her."

Speranza, though, didn't seem the least bit fazed by her employer's annoyance. She favored Elvira with a stream of unintelligible Italian, raised one hand and gave a minikarate chop to the crook of her other elbow in a universally understood gesture of disrespect, and went unhurriedly about her chores, slapping and shaping the dough on the table as unconcernedly as if such confrontations were all in a day's work.

Ignoring her, Elvira pounced on the glass of milk Cassie was sneakily trying to pour into the sink. "What is that for? Is your constitution so delicate that you cannot tolerate good Italian espresso, like the rest of us?"

So she *hadn't* heard about the baby! Cassie almost sagged with relief, but it quickly turned to dismay when Elvira tossed the same question at Speranza, this time in Italian. Without a moment's hesitation, the old servant flung back a reply, and among the words she spat at her employer, *bambino* rang loud and all too clear through the room.

As the import of what she heard sank home, Elvira grew so still and quiet, she might have been turned to stone. Outwardly, Cassie pretty much did the same, although her heart was flopping around behind her ribs like a landed fish. Otherwise, not a sound disturbed the utter silence, except for the ticking of the big old clock on the wall, and the rhythmic thump and slap of the dough hitting the tabletop.

Finally, Cassie could stand the tension no longer. "Well, now you know what Benedict and I have been trying to hide from you, though why we ever bothered is beyond me," she said, and went to leave, even though that meant stepping closer to Elvira than she'd have liked.

She wasn't normally given to wild imaginings, but there was something about the woman that made her skin crawl. Even at her best, Elvira was strange. At her worst, as now, she was outright chilling.

"*Sciatonna!*" she hissed, making no attempt to move out of the doorway as Cassie approached. "*Slut!*"

Heart still hammering, Cassie brushed by her, intending to go to the suite. Its heavy furniture and gloomy draperies might not make it her favorite place, but at least it offered some sort of sanctuary. Elvira never ventured up there, instead preferring to confine herself to the two lower floors.

Today, however, she seemed as anxious for Cassie's

company as Cassie was to be rid of hers, and kept pace with her as she climbed the stairs. Exasperated, Cassie stopped on the first landing and spun around to face her.

"Leave me alone!" she cried, past caring about keeping the peace a moment longer. "I've got nothing more to say to you."

"But I have much to say to you," Elvira taunted, her eyes blazing. "You think to trap my son with this child you claim is his, but it will take more than such a ploy to tie him to you."

"I'm not tying him against his will, Elvira. He *chooses* to be with me."

She tried to push past, but Elvira blocked her passage. "He longs to be free of you! Why else do you think he spends as much time as possible away from this house? He cannot wait to escape your incessant neediness."

"I have never once tried to keep him from attending to business."

"No?" Elvira clutched both fists to her chest in a melodramatic gesture of pleading. "Oh, Benedict," she chanted, her voice rising from its usual contralto to a maddening parody of Cassie's lighter tone, "I'd so love to spend an afternoon with you at the Museo Nazionale in Reggio Calabria…. Benedict, your sister tells me there are some marvelous Byzantine ruins in the area. When are you going to take me to see them…? Show me where you went to school, Benedict…where you played with other boys your age."

She dropped her hands and assumed her usual tone. "And so it goes," she sneered, "day after day, hour after hour!"

"Did it never occur to you that I'm merely showing an interest in my husband's birthplace, and trying to learn something of his life before he met me?"

"Rubbish! It is all about you. You want to be catered to, you spoilt child. But Benedict does not need a child for a wife. He needs a woman."

"Does he really! Someone like Giovanna, I suppose?"

"Not someone *like* her." Elvira's direct look was honest in its enmity. "Simply *her*."

"But Giovanna doesn't want to be with him. Unlike you, she respects our marriage."

"She understands him. She *knows* him, in ways you never will. She completes him. But you…you pull him apart."

Was it true? Did she whine and complain all the time? Ask too much? Perhaps give too little?

Suddenly uncertain, Cassie said haltingly, "It's never been my intention to do that. I just want—"

Elvira advanced on her, mouth pulled back in a horrible facsimile of a smile. "You want everything, all the time! You want him all to yourself, but he is not yours to have. He never will be!"

"Stop it!" Cassie cried, chilled to the bone by that manic stare, that poisonous, implacable hatred. "If Benedict knew the things you're saying—"

Elvira loomed closer. "Yes?" She planted both hands squarely against Cassie's shoulders and gave a sharp push. "What then, *americana?*"

Stumbling from the unexpected contact, Cassie reached behind to steady herself on the banister. But she'd stepped too close to the edge of the landing and instead found herself clutching at thin air.

In horrific slow motion, she felt her body tilt off balance and swing backward down the stairs. She heard a scream and thought it must be hers because, above her on the landing, Elvira stood with her mouth closed, watching composedly.

The stone banister lacerated her knuckles as Cassie fought to retain her balance. Her groin stretched painfully as one leg became hooked between two balusters, while the other continued its perilous downward slide. But, merciful heaven, it slowed her fall enough that she managed to grab hold of another baluster, and come to rest in an ungainly heap about a quarter of the way down the staircase.

Shaken to the core, she whispered, "*Good grief,* Elvira, you could have killed me!"

Face expressionless and eyes frighteningly blank, Elvira started down the stairs toward her, and for the space of a horror-filled second, Cassie thought the woman intended to finish off what she'd started.

She did not. She stared straight ahead, stepped over Cassie with the casual disregard any sane person might display toward an ant, and disappeared into her office at the rear of the lower hall.

Shivering all over, Cassie remained with her arms wrapped around the baluster, afraid to move in case she did herself more harm than good—and terrified for the well-being of her baby.

At last, and mostly because she was even more afraid that Elvira might return, she eased herself to her feet. Despite a lingering soreness at her ribs and the throbbing ache in her groin, she appeared little the worse for wear. But the baby...?

A fresh wave of horror washed over her, fueled by shock and fear of the unknown. How susceptible to injury was a fetus at this stage of pregnancy? Could a sharp blow cause brain damage? Spinal deformity?

"Oh, Benedict!" she mourned, feeling so alone that

the tears poured down her face as reaction to the whole ghastly incident set in. "Why aren't you here when I need you so badly?"

But the fact remained, he wasn't, which meant it was up to her to protect their child. And the only way to do that, she realized sorrowfully, was to remove herself permanently from a situation which had deteriorated from unpleasant, to downright dangerous.

Even though it broke her heart to leave Benedict after she'd promised him she'd stay, the baby mattered more. And that being so, she had to get herself out of this hell house and seek medical advice. She needed to find a doctor skilled enough to assess the progress of her pregnancy, and determine whether she was fit enough to make the long journey back home—and with the ability to communicate his findings to her in English.

Then, once assured that it was safe for her to travel, she'd be on the first flight back to the U.S., half a world away from her deranged mother-in-law. Enough was enough! She'd had all she could take of Elvira Constantino.

To carry out her plan, though, she had to get herself to Reggio Calabria, and there was only one way she could do that. Making her way up the second set of stairs, she let herself into the suite, made sure her passport and wallet were in her handbag, then opened the top drawer of Benedict's dresser, praying that she'd find there what she desperately needed, to carry out her plans.

Dusty and tired, Benedict drew up to the low arch leading to what had once been the Constantino stables. They'd been converted long ago to a vast garage for housing the farm vehicles, with a section at one end reserved for the family autos.

Nudging the truck into its customary spot beside the east wall, he jumped down from the cab. The sound of the door slamming closed boomed through the empty building like a cannon shot, then faded into silence.

Although the air of desertion about the place did not at first strike him as unusual—his mother and Francesca were probably still at work in the office wing, and Cassandra was most likely down on the beach enjoying the afternoon sun—still, as he turned to leave, something tugged at his brain, begging for attention. Something about the garage that wasn't quite the way it should be....

He slowed on his way out, waiting for whatever was amiss to register more fully, but when it did not, he shrugged and headed for the house. If it was a matter of importance, it would come to him later.

He'd been gone four days. Most of that time he'd spent in mountainous *la 'ndrangheta* territory, trying to broker an agreement with Angelo Menghi, leader of a gang of outlaws who hid out in the network of caves found in the area. Angelo's younger brother, Darius, was the man Elvira hired when the foreman who'd worked for the family for nearly twenty years decided he'd had enough of her misguided rule.

Darius, though, had been an unwise choice from the first. Sly, shiftless and without conscience, he'd undermined what little stability remained with the rest of the Constantino employees, and when Elvira fired him for insurrection, his swift and malevolent retaliation had been a foregone conclusion.

Benedict had no doubt that Darius was behind the vandalism which had taken such a toll on the fruit orchards, and was equally certain he'd been aided and abetted by Angelo and his lawless affiliates.

Having to negotiate with such scum had left a very sour taste in Benedict's mouth, but he knew there was only one way to put an end to the situation, and that was through negotiation. So he'd held his nose, metaphorically speaking, and done what had to be done. Now, having succeeded, all he wanted was a long, cleansing shower, a bottle of good wine, a meal, and an evening spent with Cassandra.

He had missed her, not so much during the day, when tracking down Angelo Menghi and effecting some sort of armistice had been uppermost in his mind. But at night, lying under the bright stars, he'd thought of her soft, warm body and her sweet generous mouth, and been glad of the cold mountain air stealing inside his sleeping bag.

He'd heard her voice in the murmur of the wind, smelled the perfume of her skin in the wild flowers clustered in rocky ridges of the lower slopes. He was impatient to see her again; to hold her, however tame the embrace had to be, and bury his face in her hair. To feel the mound of their growing child pressing against his belly.

But when he emerged fresh from his shower, the third-floor suite was still empty, and so, as he went down to the main floor, was the rest of the palazzo. At least, it appeared so, at first glance. And that's when it struck him that the atmosphere was *too* still, *too* silent.

He wasn't a man prone to superstition. Dealing in tangibles as he did—contracts, shipments, excise duties, import restrictions, all defined by cold, hard facts and figures—he couldn't afford to be. But, at that moment of awareness, an irrational sense of foreboding stole over him.

Suddenly, he was striding from room to room, calling

out—Cassandra's name, Francesca's, his mother's—and hearing only the echo of his own voice responding.

He came across Elvira in the salon, purely by accident. She sat stiffly in one of the high-backed chairs facing the sea, and appeared completely oblivious of her surroundings, or him.

"Mother?" He approached her cautiously; touched her hand where it rested on the carved wooden arm of the chair. "Can you hear me?"

She didn't respond, instead remaining so immobile that, for a shocking moment, he thought she might be dead. Then her eyelids fluttered in a blink, and he saw the rise and fall of her chest as she drew in a faint, trembling breath.

So quietly that he had to stoop to hear her, she said, "I am afraid of growing old and becoming useless, Benedict."

"You're fifty-nine," he told her. "Hardly in your dotage yet!"

She pinched the bridge of her nose. Spread her fingers, fanlike, across her brow and buried their tips in her hair. "But inside my head here, my mind doesn't always work. Sometimes, it seems not to know…things it should know."

His uneasiness grew. He'd never heard her sound so defeated, so utterly unsure. "Are you ill, Mother?"

"Not I. Cassandra, though…!" She covered her mouth with shaking fingers, but not soon enough to stop a little moan of anguish. "I think she's hurt, Benedict. She fell down the stairs. I think I pushed her."

His heart jolted laboriously and when he spoke, his voice seemed to roar from a great distance. "For the love of God, *why?*"

"I can't remember," she said, lifting piteous eyes to his.

Hanging on to his sanity by a thread, he tried to speak more calmly. "Where is she now, Mother?"

Elvira lifted her shoulders in a ghost of shrug. Of what? Indifference? Ignorance?

Neither was tolerable, and in a sudden overwhelming rush of fury, he grabbed her by the shoulders. Only by dint of extraordinary self-control did he restrain himself from shaking the truth out of her. "Answer me, Elvira! *Where is my wife?*"

"I looked and couldn't find her," she replied vaguely. "She's not here."

Not here...!

Like a camera lens clicking sharply into focus, his mother's words gave shape to his earlier niggling sense of something being amiss. *The place where he always parked the Lamborghini had stood empty when he rolled the truck into the garage!*

Sweat prickled his skin and he turned cold all over. If Cassandra, hurt and distraught, had driven the powerful car over the treacherous, unfamiliar coastal roads, she could be lying at the bottom of a cliff, broken or burned beyond recognition.

Anguished, desperate, he turned again to his mother. "Where's Francesca? Could she have taken Cassandra to the village to see a doctor?"

Before Elvira could answer, a door opened somewhere in the main hall and Francesca called out cheerfully, "Hello? Anyone home?"

A moment later, she appeared at the threshold of the salon. "Uh-oh," she muttered, taking in the scene in one sweeping glance, "now what's happened?"

He knew how it must look—their mother slumped in

a chair with him towering over her, so consumed with anxiety and rage that he was practically frothing at the mouth. Controlling himself with an effort, he turned away and addressed his next remark to his sister.

"Elvira claims she pushed Cassandra down the stairs," he said tightly. "Can you, by any chance, shed some light on this?"

He didn't need a verbal response. Francesca's open-mouthed shock spoke volumes, and pain clutched at his heart—a dry, bloodless, self-inflicted wound. As easily as he'd found Cassandra, he'd lost her. He'd brought her here against his better judgment, then kept her at a distance when he should have held her close. And it might have cost her her life.

Spinning on his heel, he made for the door.

Francesca found her voice. "Benedict, wait! Where are you going?"

"Where do you think? To look for my wife—and I pray to God that I find her and our child alive."

"Child?" Francesca did a double-take. "Cassandra's pregnant, and you never said anything?"

"Don't start in on me," he warned, brushing past her. "Right now, I'm in no mood to justify anything to anyone. I've got bigger things to worry about."

"Such as rampaging through the countryside like a madman?" She caught his arm. "Stop and think for a minute! Cassandra might not have gone anywhere. She might be resting upstairs."

"She's not. She's nowhere in this house, and my car's gone from the garage."

Francesca paled, but clung to reason regardless. "Then we start by phoning the police. There aren't too many red Lamborghini Diablos in the area. If she's driving around out there, she'll be easy enough to spot."

"And if she's not?" He cast a savage glance at his mother, who sat with her head pressed against the back of the chair, and her eyes closed. As if, by her refusing to look, what she'd done would miraculously cease to exist!

"We'll call the local clinic, and Dr. Vieri's office," Francesca said. "Stop expecting the worst and think about it, Benedict! If she'd been in an accident, we'd have heard about it before now. It's just a matter of alerting the authorities and waiting for them to track her down. But if she decides to come back on her own, I think she'd feel a lot safer if she found you here waiting for her."

It was no more in his nature to hand over control of his affairs to someone else, than he'd thought it was in his mother's to physically attack his wife. Yet what Francesca said made sense. Better to cast as wide an official search net as possible while some daylight remained. Because if he didn't have news of Cassandra by sunset, he didn't know how he'd face the coming night.

Cassie stepped out into the late-afternoon clamor of the city, and inhaled deeply and luxuriously. For the first time in hours, her lungs were unconstricted by fear and, despite the stench of exhaust fumes, the air smelled incomparably sweet.

Her baby was alive and well. She had heard his heart beat; seen it on the ultrasound screen.

Behind her stood the hospital, no longer a site of potential threat to everything she held dear, but a benign, comforting presence designed to protect her. After compiling a thorough case history, and taking a battery of tests including a sonogram, the chief obstetrician on staff had told her, "*Signora*, your baby is in excellent health, as are you. The fall has left you with a bruise or two, but the pregnancy is not in danger.''

''And my cervix?''

''Is entirely as it should be at this stage. You and your husband may relax.'' Eyes twinkling, he'd patted her hand. ''He will be happy to hear this, yes?''

''Yes.''

But Benedict was out of touch, somewhere in the mountains of the interior, and much though she wished it could be otherwise, she had no intention of going back to the palazzo to wait for his return. If Elvira wanted a second shot at disposing of her daughter-in-law, she'd have to travel to San Francisco to get it.

As it turned out, the earliest Cassie could book a flight home was the following afternoon, but even that didn't cast a cloud on her spirits. For the first time in weeks, she was free of the looming, gloomy presence of the Constantino estate and only now, with the bustle and noise of traffic and people swirling around her, did she realize how much she'd missed them.

Reggio Calabria might be the provincial capital, but a major earthquake early in the twentieth century had destroyed much of its antiquity, and the conglomeration of newer buildings offered little in the way of interest or beauty. Yet it possessed the sort of vitality and pulse only to be found in a city, and she relished it.

Consulting the tourist map she'd purchased, she located a hotel on a quiet side street. Though not ostentatious, it nevertheless had a certain charm. The room she was shown was clean, comfortable, had its own bathroom and a telephone, and looked out over a small rear garden set with umbrella-shaded tables. Furthermore, there was parking at the side of the building for the Lamborghini.

She sat at one of the outdoor tables, and with the help of her phrase book, ordered a vanilla milkshake. Afterward, since she had nothing with her but a small cosmetic kit and the clothes she stood up in, she drove in search of a place to buy such basics as shampoo and toothpaste, and a change of underwear.

After making her purchases, she followed a different route on the way back to the hotel, and passed by a little boutique specializing in maternity wear. Confident now that she'd carry her baby to term, and free to let the whole world know it, she went inside and bought two outfits. One was a dress in silk the color of almond blossom, the other a royal-blue cotton two-piece.

By the time she returned to her room, the sun lay low in the west and kerosene lamps flared in the garden to ward off the shadows of dusk. Relaxed for the first time in what seemed like forever, she bathed, put on her new blue outfit and, lured by the tempting aromas rising from the kitchen below her open window, went down for dinner.

Ravenous, she dined on wonderful olives, and bread warm from the oven; on swordfish and pasta stuffed with eggplant; on local cheese and fruit. The only thing missing was not having Benedict there to share the experience, and she missed him dreadfully.

She saw the moon rise and listened to someone nearby playing a violin. She watched two lovers at another table—how they gazed at one another, and held hands. And again, the ache of missing Benedict took hold.

At twenty-two minutes past three the next morning, she awoke to a sensation in her womb as if a butterfly had swept open its wings. A moment later, it happened again, and she realized her baby was moving.

She wished Benedict was there to share the moment

with her. But he was not, so she settled for the next best thing. Sitting up, she reached for the phone on the bedside table and called Trish.

It was six o'clock the next morning—more than fourteen hours since he'd learned she'd gone missing—before the phone rang and released Benedict from the confines of hell.

"She's been found," the local police chief informed him. "She's registered at a hotel in Reggio Calabria. We were able to track her down through the car. Just as well you provided us with a full description, otherwise we'd still be looking."

He was on the road within fifteen minutes, the hotel name and address scribbled on a slip of paper beside him on the seat. Traffic was light and he made good time, arriving in the provincial capital before the morning rush began.

The hotel stood on a quiet side street. The desk clerk confirmed that Cassandra had taken a room and had not yet checked out. Benedict did a quick sweep of the lobby, locating the stairs, the dining room, and the door to the courtyard, to be sure he had all points of entry and exit covered, then took up his post in a corner near the front desk which commanded a clear view of the entire lobby.

She didn't show up until almost half-past nine, by which time he was beginning to worry that she'd somehow slipped through his fingers again, or else was too indisposed to make it out of bed. Just as he was about to demand a key to her room, however, she came down the stairs, dog-eared phrase book in hand.

She looked rested and lovely and reassuringly pregnant. Glowing on the outside from the sun, and on the inside with a serenity he found hard to understand, given her trauma of the previous day. He knew without having to ask, that the baby was fine.

Unaware that she was being observed, she made straight for the garden. Not about to let her out of his sight, Benedict followed and watched as she chose a table in the corner, next to a small wall fountain, popped a pair of sunglasses on her nose, and studied the menu.

The tables on either side were unoccupied. Unobtrusively sliding onto the chair directly behind hers, he leaned back and said over his shoulder, "You seem familiar with the hotel, *signorina*. What do you recommend I order for breakfast?"

She let out a sighing little squeak of recognition, a captivating sound reminiscent of the one she made when she approached orgasm, then recovered enough to say primly, "I'm a *signora*. A married lady."

"And I," he said, "am a married man in dire straits. My wife, you see, has run off, and I'm desperate to find her."

"What did you do to drive her away?"

"I'm afraid I neglected her shamefully, and in doing so, exposed her to danger in the one place she ought to have been safe. Should something untoward happen to her, I don't know how I'll live with myself."

"Does she know how strongly you feel?"

"I'm not sure. I've never actually said so, mostly because I didn't fully realize it myself until yesterday, when I lost her."

"Women need to be told, *signor*. They need to hear the words."

"Have I left it too late to convince her?"

She didn't reply and he, in a wave of uncertainty as demoralizing as it was foreign, dropped his arm to his side and reached back his hand toward her. He knew she couldn't see the gesture; knew it was a puny, even cowardly way to try to mend what was broken between them. Because she was right: actions didn't always speak louder than words; sometimes, it was the other way around.

"Is she planning to come back to me, do you think?" he asked. "Or is her plan to keep on going, and make a life without me?"

The seconds dragged by, an eternity punctuated by an avalanche of regret for the mistakes he'd made. She'd shown him in a hundred different ways that she could love him if only he would let her, but because he hadn't been able to keep his rampant testosterone under control, he'd rebuffed her overtures.

Now, unable to tolerate the suspense, he was on the verge of accepting that the distance between them had grown too vast to bridge when, as lightly as a breath of wind, the tips of her fingers brushed against his and caught hold.

"I think she'd far rather be with her husband," she said.

CHAPTER TEN

"IT'S NOT that I wanted to leave you, Benedict. It's that I didn't feel I had a choice," she said, when she could speak past the emotion clogging her throat. "Not that I blame you for what happened yesterday," she added quickly. "You're not responsible for your mother's actions."

Without letting go of her hand, he left his seat and took the empty chair at her table. He wore his navy slacks and a white sports shirt with the casual elegance so typical of everything he did. Just then, though, there was nothing casual or typical about his manner. The self-possession she'd thought impregnable lay in tatters, as evidenced by the haunted shadows in his eyes.

"But I'm responsible for you," he said urgently. "I'm responsible for my child."

"You can't always be there to intercede between me and perceived danger. No one can. And in case you haven't noticed, I'm capable of looking out for myself."

"Obviously," he said drily. "A lot more so than I realized, judging by the way you escaped under your own steam. How'd you find the drive, by the way?"

"Horrendous, especially once I got here. The traffic congestion in this city is a nightmare. But the worst part was wondering if I'd be able to find your car keys at the palazzo. I knew where you usually kept them, but was so afraid you might have taken them with you when you left for the mountains. If you had, I don't know how I'd have got away." She shot him an amused glance. "But if it's the Lamborghini you're really worried about, don't be. It doesn't have a scratch on it.''

''I don't give a damn about the car, Cassandra! There are plenty more where it came from, but you…!'' He expelled a heartfelt breath. ''*You* are irreplaceable, and I never again want to come so close to losing you.''

''I already told you, Benedict, that what happened wasn't your fault.''

''Indirectly, it was,'' he insisted gravely. ''I could have acknowledged sooner that having you live under my mother's roof was a mistake. God knows, you tried to tell me, often enough. I could have sent you to Bianca. You'd have been safe with her. She'd have taken good care of you and the baby.''

''I wouldn't have gone. I wanted to be with you—at least, I did until yesterday. Then, I'm afraid, it all just became too much.'' She leaned across the table and cupped his jaw, wanting very much to erase the worry marking his features. ''But I'm so glad you came after me. I have wonderful news.''

He shook his head in disbelief, and almost smiled. ''How can you possibly mine something wonderful out of near-tragedy?''

''Easily,'' she said. ''I checked into the hospital here yesterday, just to be sure everything was as it should be with my pregnancy.''

He turned his mouth to her palm and pressed a kiss there. ''And?''

''And I heard and saw our baby's heart beating. Then, last night, I felt him move.'' Reaching into her bag, she drew out the prints from the ultrasound and passed them to him. ''Here are the first pictures of your son, Benedict.''

''We have a boy?'' His hand shook as he took them,

and she almost started crying at the look of wonder on his face as he examined the blurry images. "And he's perfect?"

"He's perfect!"

He stroked his fingertip over the glossy paper. "We're so lucky, *cara!* So blessed!"

"Yes," she said softly. "And that's not all. The problem with my cervix…well, it turned out not to be a problem, after all. The doctor gave me a clean bill of health."

"And you trust his opinion?"

"He's a specialist, Benedict. I think it's safe to assume he knows what he's talking about."

"So I have a healthy wife, as well as a healthy baby?"

"Yes."

"I wish that was enough to make me a completely happy man," he said, the joy which had illuminated his face fading into solemnity.

Her heart sank a little. "And it's not?"

"How can it be, considering everything that happened with my mother?" For the first time since she'd known him, the candor and pride always so predominant in his gaze was tinged with shame. "I hardly know what to say, Cassandra. I wish I could offer some insight into her actions, but frankly, I'm at a loss. I questioned her, of course, but she was able to give no rational explanation for her behavior. Have you any idea what possessed her?"

"I suppose I might have provoked her." Trying to be fair, Cassie explained the sequence of events. "I think finding out about the baby the way she did was what really set her off. But what shook me was that she'd willingly endanger the life of her unborn grandchild. I know she's your mother, Benedict, but I'm sorry to say I find what she did unforgivable."

"Don't apologize," he said grimly. "I never thought to see the day that I'd say this, but she is not the mother I've always known, nor even a woman. She is a monster and while I've thought for some time that she might be mentally ill, I'm now beginning to wonder if she's not criminally insane!"

He spoke with fire, but Cassie could see what it cost him. The pain in his eyes was impossible to miss, and she hated having to add to it. But he had to know that there was no going back to the way things had been.

"I wish I could disagree with you, but I can't," she said sadly. "I'm afraid I can't ever go back to the palazzo. Nor do I don't want your mother anywhere near me or my baby, ever again."

"I understand. And I wouldn't dream of asking you to return. But I am begging you not to go back to the States, not yet. Please, Cassandra, come with me instead to La Posada, my home in Sicily. We'll be alone, there, and you'll be safe. We can start over again, the way a married couple should, with a proper honeymoon."

"I'm hardly equipped to go off on a honeymoon," she protested, laughing. "I left in such a hurry that, except for a few items I bought yesterday, all my things are still at the palazzo."

"Then as soon as we've finished breakfast, we'll shop some more."

"Well, not that it doesn't sound wonderful, but what about work? You can't just walk away when your entire family is depending on you."

"Yes, I can," he said, gripping her hands so firmly, she almost winced. "You and our baby are my family, now. I won't say I don't care about my sisters and, yes, even my mother. But I'm through with putting other people, other things, ahead of you and me, Cassandra. From here on, our marriage comes first.''

He spoke with feeling. With controlled desire. The atmosphere shimmered with the promise of unfettered passion waiting to be allayed, of a future suddenly bright with promise of the happy-ever-after she'd always longed for.

And if all that didn't quite add up to the same as *I love you, Cassandra,* it came close and, after the tumult and trauma of the last twenty-four hours, for now, for Cassie, it was enough.

He took her to shops she'd never have discovered on her own. Overrode her protests and spent extravagant amounts on her: an entire wardrobe of silk lingerie, shoes, perfume, and maternity dresses so pretty she could have stayed pregnant forever, just for the pleasure of wearing them.

They ate stuffed calamari and preserved figs for lunch, drank fragrant *caffe latte,* talked about his journey inland and the progress he'd made in putting the Calabrian end of the family enterprise in order again.

"I've persuaded our old foreman to come back," he told her. "Given him full control of operations. He's well respected in the village. He'll have no trouble enlisting hired hands. Many who'd defected are ready to return and start working the orchards again."

They arrived at his Sicilian hideaway late in the afternoon, and Cassie fell in love with the place on sight. If the Constantino palazzo hulked at the top of the cliff, all ancient stone and somber, brooding confinement, Benedict's home, situated on a gentle slope of land running down to the shore, flowed in a graceful curve of white stucco walls and blue tiled roof around a turquoise swimming pool.

Brilliant flowering shrubs filled every nook and cranny of the garden. Fountains splashed and little streams ran under rocks to form tiny hidden pools where brightly colored fish darted back and forth.

He led her on a tour of the place. The windows and doors were wide, allowing the breeze to sweep the house with the scent of the jasmine growing in a planter beside the front entrance. The rooms were spacious and airy and, during the day, filled with the rippling reflection of sunlight glimmering on the sea.

Marble, smooth as silk, covered the floors. Instead of stiff, uncomfortable carved chairs and sofas upholstered in heavy plush, leather couches, puffy and soft as marshmallows, graced the salon. The dining table was a sheet of beveled glass supported on a finely wrought iron base, the chairs pale wood with seats covered in white linen.

The master suite was huge, with floor-to-ceiling windows opening onto a private terrace, a charming sitting area at one end and, oddly, two enormous bathrooms accessed by dressing rooms.

"If you're wondering how many other women I've brought here," Benedict said, noticing her surprise at the convenient his-and-hers arrangement, "you're the first— and last. I didn't design this house, Cassandra. I bought it three years ago, for the location and view, from a couple who moved to an apartment in Roma to be near their grandchildren. That it happens to be designed for a man and his wife is purely and conveniently coincidental."

Embarrassed that he'd picked up on her thoughts with such uncanny accuracy, she replied, "You didn't have to tell me that."

"Yes, I did," he said. "There've been enough clouds hanging over us. I won't allow there to be any more. You're my lady, *cara,* and the only mistress, ever, of my house."

As the sun set, he left her to bathe and dress at leisure, his parting glance telling her that soon, very soon, there would be nothing keeping them apart. Not the walls of her bathroom, not the clothes on her body, and never again the sullen, forbidding presence of his mother tainting the atmosphere. The knowledge left her quivering with anticipation.

That night, they dined by candlelight on a terrace overlooking the sea, with the murmur of the waves falling in soft cadence against the shore, and the moon riding low on the horizon. Music drifted from the house, old songs from the 1940s, full of lost love found again and two hearts beating as one. Carmine, the chef, served veal Parmigiano and rollentini, with a light salad to start and chilled *zabaglione* for dessert.

And throughout, with every word, every glance, every touch, undercurrents of expectancy rippled between her and Benedict, an unseen but insistent third party refusing to go denied.

Sipping a small flute of celebratory champagne, Cassie sat across from her husband, conscious of time ticking toward the sexual finale of a union now nearly four and a half months old. The flicker of candle flames showcased his high cheekbones and swathed his dark eyes in mystery. Weeks of strenuous physical labor had sculpted his already well-toned body to hard perfection and deepened his olive skin to bronze.

He looked handsome as a god, and she wished she could fast-freeze the perfection of the moment—of him—and keep them as a talisman against future assaults on their marriage. Because for all Cassie's stated intention to remain as far away from his mother as possible, the reality was that as long as Elvira was alive, the specter of her destructive potential remained a dark cloud on the horizon.

"What are you thinking about, *cara?*" Benedict asked, eyeing her lazily over the rim of his wineglass.

"I'm wondering how you can bear to leave such a place. It's exquisite here."

He smiled, and pulling her to her feet, led her over the flagstones in a dreamy waltz. "I'm happy you think so because it's *my* favorite retreat, also. The Manhattan apartment is comfortable and works well as a base for North American business, and those in Paris, London and Hong Kong serve me well enough. But this is where I come when I need to unwind."

Stunned by the casual way he rattled off his real estate holdings, as if having *pieds à terre* scattered over three continents was standard for any man, she lost the rhythm of the waltz and almost stepped on his foot. "Exactly how many homes do you own?"

"Just four," he said, not missing a beat. "My work involves a fair bit of travel, and I don't care for hotels."

Apparently not! "And boats?"

"Two—the motor launch that brought us here from the mainland, and a fifty-four foot sailing sloop I keep in the Caribbean."

She swallowed. "Um… at the risk of sounding incredibly crass, are you *very* rich, Benedict?"

"I suppose." He shrugged carelessly and stroked his hand up her spine. "Why? Does it matter?"

"Only insofar as I feel like a fool," she said, staring, mortified, over his shoulder. "You must have laughed yourself silly when I offered you money to help cover the losses brought on by your mother's business mishaps. I thought, when you talked of having to find another way to make a living, that you were in financial straits.''

"I didn't laugh, Cassandra," he murmured. "I was very touched by your generosity."

"Even so, it shows how much we still don't know about each other."

Slowing to the point that they were doing little more than sway in each other's arms, he brushed his mouth over the crown of her head and pulled her close enough that she could feel every line of his torso delineated against hers. "But we have the rest of our lives to learn, yes?"

"Yes," she agreed, his nearness creating alarming repercussions within her. To an onlooker, he might have appeared completely relaxed and in control, but up this close, his body told a different story.

"Perhaps," he said, not sounding quite so composed, after all, "we should start this journey of discovery very soon. I have waited a very long time to be a proper husband to you, Cassandra, and I am not known for my patience."

The smoky timbre of his voice sent a flash of heat streaking through her that left her trembling. "Then perhaps," she suggested, "you should take me to bed, before we make a public display of ourselves out here, in front of your house staff."

He needed no second urging. Sweeping her into his arms, he strode across the terrace and through the house to the master suite. "I like a woman who speaks her mind plainly," he said. "I like *you*, my Cassandra. I like you very much."

CHAPTER ELEVEN

HE'D orchestrated the entire night with such strict attention to detail that he actually thought it would happen exactly as planned—that he could tame his body and bring to this, the real start of their marriage, the subtlety and restraint that would allow both Cassandra and himself to savor every second.

It did not happen so. He was too hungry and she was too fine, too lovely and too giving. Barely had they reached the bedroom before raw need vanquished any notions of finesse. The way she breathed his name in his ear, the whisper of satiny underthings shifting against her skin, the soft, full curves of her pregnancy, her hand playing over his chest...there were too many temptations. Assaulted on every front, he was ready to burst.

Kicking closed the door behind him, he brought his mouth down on hers in the kind of kiss he hadn't dared allow before because it imitated too closely the act of love. The way she welcomed him, opening her mouth to his tongue, and moaning softly, should have staved off the wild craving long enough for him to carry her as far as the bed.

It did not.

Driven wild by the scent and taste of her, and with his mouth still fastened to hers, he lowered her to the floor, slowly enough that there wasn't an inch of her that didn't slither provocatively over him. Half-blind with need, he worked the buttons of her dress open, pushed it aside, and dragged his lips lower. To her throat, where her pulse beat as frantically as the wings of a trapped bird. To her breasts, barely contained by her lacy bra.

She whimpered when he took her nipple lightly between his teeth and rolled his tongue around it. And whimpered again, more helplessly, when he slid her dress high up her thighs. She wore no stockings underneath, just panties, and the patch of fabric between her legs was damp.

Edging it aside, he buried his finger in her soft, warm flesh. She quivered at his touch, so ready for him, so hot and moist and tight, that he almost came.

Wanting to prolong the pleasure, he attempted to put a little distance between them, but she arched against him, and clenched her thighs together, hard, to imprison his hand. Ran both of hers down his chest to his waist, and his belt. Tore open the buckle, unzipped his fly, and boldly thrust inside to cup the pulsing, heavy weight of his erection in her palm.

It was game over then. Within seconds, they were tearing at each other's clothing until they stood naked. The bed lay only five meters away, but it might as well have been a kilometer or more. There was no way he could cover the distance. No way he could hold back the encroaching tide long enough to allow the mattress to accommodate them.

Spinning her around, he pinned her against the wall, hooked his hands beneath her buttocks, and lifted her. She wrapped her legs around his waist and rested the mound of their unborn child against his belly.

"Are you sure…it's safe to do this?" Teetering on the point of no return, he fought his way past the passion smoking through his body, and dragged the question from his tortured lungs.

Her fingers gouged at his shoulders; urged him to completion. "Very sure," she whispered.

It was as well. He was, after all, but a man, as subject to human weakness as the next. And she was temptation personified.

For a breathtaking nanosecond of sheer, exquisite torment, he allowed his aroused flesh to tease hers, nudging and retreating from the eager folds of her femininity until she was begging him, in broken little cries, to put an end to her misery.

Then, at last…at long last…he was inside her. Moving with her. Thrusting in rhythm, back and forth. Feeling her close around him, strong and silken and hot. And for all that he wanted to take her in long, easy strokes, it was not to be. Responsive to every nuance of his seduction, she clutched handfuls of his hair, and burst into tears as the climax she tried so hard to delay swept over her in wracking spasms no man could withstand.

Sweat blurring his vision, he braced one hand against the door and, with a mighty groan, gave himself up to an explosion of sensation so intense, he thought it would kill him.

It robbed him of his soul.

Left him shaking and depleted.

Left him so strung out and defenseless that, with the aftershocks of orgasm still rumbling through his body, he uttered words he'd never before said to any woman. *"Ah, Cassandra, mi tesoro, te amo!"*

"What did you say?" she panted, raising dazed eyes to his.

"I love you," he said. "You are my life, and I will never again put any other ahead of you."

She wept again then, not with volatile sobs which had shaken her before, but with quiet containment. Tears filmed her lovely blue eyes and trembled from her lashes. "Oh, Benedict!" she sighed brokenly. "I've waited so long to hear you say those words. Waited so long to say them to you. Because I have loved you for a long time now, and I was so afraid you'd never love me back."

"Don't be afraid, *mi amore,*" he told her. "The bad times are behind us, and I give you my word there will be nothing but golden days ahead."

For five days, she believed him. For five days and nights, he devoted himself to pleasing her. The utter perfection of that time made the long wait for their honeymoon worth every painful second which had preceded it.

He made love to her often. With tenderness, and with unrestrained passion. Playfully, with laughter, and soberly, with heartfelt, murmured endearments. They came together in the swimming pool early in the day, with the sun just high enough to tint La Posada's white stucco walls pink; and on the beach at midnight, with only the stars to witness their pleasure.

Waking before him one morning, she watched him sleeping, all long, loose-limbed elegance, with his dark hair falling in disarray over his brow. Unable to help herself, she leaned over and pressed a featherlight kiss to his shoulder. Just enough to steal the taste of him, but not enough to disturb him.

But when she raised her head, his eyes were open and full of lazy laughter. He crooked a finger at her, and in a sleep-gravelly voice said, "Come here, wench."

"Yes, master," she purred, sliding on top of him.

"Buon giorno, mi amore," he murmured, thrusting up to meet her.

* * *

He showed her Sicily. Took her to Palermo, to little, out-of-the-way *trattorias,* and introduced her to traditional Sicilian foods like cuttlefish served in its own black ink, and the best veal Marsala she'd ever eaten. Tempted her with Sicilian *gelato* and almond marzipan pastries colored and shaped to resemble fruit. Showed her palatial homes, Byzantine and Romanesque Gothic churches.

One day, when they were out in the country, they met the family and friends of a bride escorting her in a procession from her parents' home to the village church, where the groom waited with his mother and other witnesses. This led to Benedict's explaining the phenomenon of *Mammismo,* common throughout Italy but especially prevalent in Sicily, in which men maintained such close ties to their mothers that their first loyalty, always, was to *Mammina* instead of their own wives.

"But not in your case," Cassie said, secure in his love. "You'd never put your mother first."

"No, never," he replied, grabbing her in a fierce hug. "I am Italian by birth, but North American in outlook."

It all came to an end on the sixth day, beginning with a phone call from Francesca. She was so beside herself that, even though Benedict took the call, Cassie could hear her sister-in-law's distressed voice from clear across the room. Benedict's expression was thunderous when he finally hung up the phone, and that Elvira was at the root of whatever crisis had arisen came as no surprise to Cassie.

"You have to go back there, don't you?" she said hollowly, a leaden dismay sinking to the pit of her stomach, and leaving her shivering despite the day's brilliant heat.

"*Si!*" He practically spat out the word. "But this time, I promise you, Cassandra, I will put a stop to the nonsense, once and for all. I will not allow Elvira to continue creating upheaval in all our lives.''

''I don't know how you'll stop her. She doesn't live by other people's rules.''

''I'll find a way,'' he said, framing her face between his hands, and scouring her features with his gaze. ''One way or another, I promise you this will end. If I have to, I'll have her committed. God knows, she's giving every indication she's losing her mind!''

''Even if you do, I won't come with you, Benedict. I sympathize with your dilemma. I even recognize this isn't something Francesca can manage alone. But I *absolutely refuse* to expose myself or our baby to further jeopardy.''

''Nor will I ask you to.'' He pulled her hard against him, close enough that she could feel the furious thud of his heart. ''I will send you to Bianca, instead.''

''No,'' she said. ''There's no telling how long you'll be tied up this time, and I've already stayed away from my business interests weeks longer than I originally intended. If I can't be with you—and it would seem, yet again, that I cannot—then I'm going home.''

He held her tighter and drew in a savage breath. ''I can't bear to think of you being so far away!''

''I don't consider it an ideal solution, either. But all other considerations apart, I'm not being fair to Trish, leaving her to handle my workload, as well as her own. Much though I like Bianca and her family, my life isn't with them, nor is it here, in this country.''

Releasing her, he paced the length of the room and stared out of the window, his spine rigid, his shoulders tense. ''You're my wife, Cassandra!'' he finally burst out, spinning back to face her. ''You belong with me! This shouldn't be happening to us, not now, not when we've just given our marriage a fighting chance to succeed. Can we not arrive at some sort of compromise that will allow us to remain together?''

His misery tore at her, but not enough to weaken her resolve. ''I refuse to subject myself to more of your mother's abuse. I'm sorry, Benedict, really I am, but she crossed a line with me when she pushed me down the stairs. There's no going back on something like that.''

''Then how about this? Tomorrow, let me put you on a flight to *Milano*. Stay with Bianca and give me until the weekend to clean up this latest mess. Three days I'm asking for, *cara*. You can give me that, can't you?''

''And what if you can't work things out that soon? How long, Benedict, do I put *my* interests on hold while you take care of yours?''

''Three more days only.'' Picking up the phone, he punched in a number and carried out a rapid-fire conversation with whoever answered. ''So,'' he said, hanging up finally and turning again to her, ''we have tickets on a flight leaving *Milano* at three on Friday afternoon. I'll meet you in the departure lounge two hours before that. By Saturday, you'll be home again.''

He made it seem possible, easy. Yet nothing involving Elvira was ever simple. She thrived on complications.

Seeing her doubt, he took her hand and crushed it to his heart. ''I promise you, Cassandra, nothing will prevent me from being beside you on that jet. On Saturday night, we'll be dining on Fisherman's Wharf. On Monday, I'll be looking for office space in San Francisco, and you'll be back among the friends you've missed, among people who love you almost as much as I do. I swear on my life, I will not allow my mother to derail our marriage a second time.''

She heard the conviction in his deep, sexy voice; saw

it in the dark, fervent glow of his eyes. And because she loved him and wanted very much to believe him, she buried her reservations and agreed to his terms. "Three days then. But if you let me down…"

He touched his finger to her mouth. "It isn't going to happen."

They left Sicily the next morning, and by midafternoon on Tuesday, she was once again in Milan. Bianca and Enrico took her into their arms, and into their hearts, with the kind of warmth she hadn't known from family since her mother's death.

"We'll make this a holiday for you," they said. "Before you know it, Friday will have arrived and so will Benedict. Never doubt him, Cassandra. He is a man of his word."

That night, he phoned to make sure she'd arrived safely and to give her a progress report. He'd arranged for Elvira to be admitted to hospital in Reggio Calabria the next day, for a full physical and psychiatric assessment.

Regardless of the outcome, her reign of terror was over because Pasquale Renaldo, Francesca's high school sweetheart, had asked her to marry him. He was a good man. He'd worked his own family's bergamot orchards since graduating from college and was well able to take over the running of the Constantino estate.

"Te amo, Cassandra," Benedict told Cassie, at the end of the call. "I'll see you on Friday."

On Wednesday, he phoned with another update. He'd be arriving in Milan at ten-thirty on Friday morning, leaving him plenty of time to make the international flight. He was meeting with Elvira's doctors tomorrow, to learn of their findings, and was determined to enforce whatever treatment they prescribed for her.

Before hanging up, he said again, "*Te amo, cara mia. Only two more nights apart*, and then we're together forever."

On Thursday, he didn't phone, but Cassie tried to accept Bianca's explanation that turning over the family operation to Pasquale would be a long and complicated process, particularly in light of Elvira's mishandling of so many aspects of the business. Still, the hours dragged and no matter how hard Cassie tried, little tendrils of uneasiness uncurled inside her like evil snakes eating away at her optimism. Not until Benedict was by her side and they were miles away, would she really believe the nightmare was over.

At last, Friday arrived. Simmering with pent-up anxiety, she arrived at Malpensa airport in time to meet his flight from Calabria. But although the commuter jet disgorged a vast number of passengers, Benedict was not among them.

"We must not have noticed him," Bianca said, slipping an encouraging arm around Cassie's shoulders. "Don't forget, he was expecting to meet you in the international departure lounge, not here. Because he's in transit, he might have gone there by a different route, and is already waiting for you."

But he was not. Nor did anyone answer when Bianca phoned the palazzo to find out if he had, in fact, been on the flight in the first place. "But that's a good sign," she insisted, steadfastly refusing to admit the unthinkable—that he simply wasn't going to show. "Francesca's probably helping Pasquale get used to his new job, and Benedict's already here, probably buying you something exquisite in the duty-free shop. Either that, or he's missed his flight. But if he has, he'll be on the next one, and you've still got four hours before you leave—plenty of time, Cassandra, really!''

''Why don't I believe you?'' Cassie said, so miserably furious that she could barely speak.

Ever the loyal twin, Bianca said staunchly, ''I know he won't let you down. Trust him, Cassandra.''

She *had* trusted him, time and again. She'd married him, on trust; let him spirit her halfway around the world, on trust. Against her better judgment, she'd remained in his crazy mother's home when every instinct told her she should leave. She'd entrusted him with her life, and with her child's.

Most of all, she'd trusted him to keep his last promise to her. But he had not, and when the final boarding call came over the loudspeakers for passengers traveling on Delta Airlines Flight 7602, to New York JFK, she knew what she had to do.

''Leave for America without him?'' Bianca was aghast. ''But he's your husband, Cassandra! You must be here when he comes. He will expect it. It is the Italian way!''

''I don't care about the Italian way,'' she cried. ''I'm an American and from now on, I'm doing what's best for me.''

''But there will be an explanation for his actions!''

''There always is, Bianca,'' she said wearily. ''And the trouble is, there always will be. Benedict can't separate himself from this family's problems. He makes them his own. Every time something goes wrong, he feels he has to fix it.'' She picked up her carry-on bag. ''Either he shows up here in the next five minutes, or this marriage, such as it was, is over.''

He did not. When the Boeing 767-300 took off some fifteen minutes later, the seat beside her remained unoccupied.

He arrived at the international departure gate in time to see the aircraft carrying his wife lift off and head toward the west. Frustrated, breathless, exhausted, he raked weary fingers through his hair and swore softly.

"That's not going to help any," a familiar voice informed him, and he turned to find Bianca behind him, her face crumpled with misery.

The faint, unreasonable hope that Cassandra might not have boarded the jet died. "So she's gone," he said.

"She's gone." His sister, normally so calm, gave vent to her annoyance by rapping him smartly on the arm. "How could you let her down like this, Benedict, when you knew how much was riding on keeping your promise to her?"

He caught her hands. Held them firmly, knowing he was about to deal a blow she couldn't possibly be prepared for. "It couldn't be helped," he said, and related what had happened.

For a moment, she looked at him uncomprehendingly, then fell against him with a cry. "Our mother had a brain tumor?" she said, when she could control her tears. "Oh, Benedict! Is that the reason for her headaches, and her odd behavior?"

"It would appear so." He led her to a row of unoccupied seats, and waited until she'd composed herself a little before going into the details. "Fortunately, the tumor itself was benign. Removing it, though, involved delicate, potentially life-threatening surgery too complex to be performed in Calabria. She had to be flown to Rome where a team of neurosurgeons performed the operation last night."

"You're saying she underwent surgery yesterday, and I'm only now hearing about it? For pity's sake, Benedict, why? You had no right to keep this from me. Elvira is my mother, too!"

"Once we had a diagnosis, everything happened too quickly. Her headaches were warnings of a time bomb waiting to go off. If we'd waited another week to seek a medical opinion—perhaps even another day—we might have left it too late."

"Even so, a phone call to let me know—"

"Bianca, there was no time for you to get to her beforehand, so what was the point? You'd have done nothing but pace the floor all night, and fret at being too far away to be of any help. I decided it was best to wait until we knew the outcome of the operation."

"And Cassandra? She didn't deserve to be kept informed of the reason you didn't show up when you said you would?"

"I'd have told her once we were headed back to the U.S."

"Except you didn't get here in time to do that. She was very angry, and very hurt. I don't know how you're going to make this up to her."

"I do." He checked his watch and saw that nearly an hour had passed since he'd arrived in Milan. He had no time to lose, if the plan he'd conceived during the flight from Rome was to succeed. "As her only son, it was my duty to see that our mother received the treatment she needed, but I've done my part here, Bianca. The rest is up to you and Francesca. Elvira's facing a long road to recovery and needs her family's support, but I can't be the one she leans on. I have a marriage to look after, and a wife and child to care for. From now on, my first responsibility is to them."

"Of course. I understand completely." She reached up and kissed his cheek. "I can see you're impatient to be off so I'll get out of your hair. Call me with good news soon, and don't worry about a thing at this end. Francesca and I will cope."

He watched her leave, regretting having to lay such a heavy burden on her shoulders when she already had a family of her own to care for and he, in the past, had always been the one to step in when help was needed. Yet, what else could he do this time? At what point did he reclaim the right to live his own life?

He smelled of hospitals, of antiseptic chemicals; could even taste them. He needed a shower, a shave, a change of clothes, and, God knew, he needed sleep. But attending to those needs lay far down on his list of priorities. Eyes gritty with fatigue, he expelled a long breath and took out his cell phone.

"It's Benedict Constantino," he said, when the call went through. "I have to be in San Francisco before tonight. How soon can you get me there?"

He had another two hours to kill before the private jet was cleared for takeoff. Long enough to claim his luggage and take advantage of the amenities in the charter company's executive lounge. Long enough to call Cassandra's friend Trish, and enlist her help.

CHAPTER TWELVE

THROUGHOUT the long, endless journey home, Cassie tried to come to grips with her situation and decide how she was going to proceed, once she was back in familiar territory. But weariness, while not allowing her to sleep, seemed to have robbed her mind of its ability to reason. She existed in a vacuum, totally removed from everything and everyone around her.

She wished she could remain there forever. It was, in a strange, out-of-this-world sort of way, very peaceful, except for those moments when, without warning, Benedict wandered into her thoughts. Then the pain and loss besieged her on all sides.

She felt wounded. Betrayed. Robbed of joy. For a brief, lovely time, he had loved her. But not enough. Never enough. And her mind, clicking into gear, recognized that it all had to end. She couldn't keep putting herself through the mill this way. It was too destructive, too debilitating, too humiliating.

Her flight touched down in San Francisco just after seven that night, nearly an hour later than scheduled because of air traffic delays leaving JFK in New York. No one was there to meet her because she hadn't let her friends know she was returning. She was too fragile to tolerate their sympathy. All she wanted was to go home and surround herself with the things she loved—her grandmother's china, her bombé chest, her paintings, her rugs. *Things* didn't hurt. Only people could do that.

She took a taxi from the airport, paid the driver, then

stood a moment on the sidewalk and let the fact that she was home at last seep into every pore. *Now,* she could take charge of her life again.

Leaving her bags inside the lower lobby, she climbed the stairs and let herself into the town house. The place had been closed up for nearly four months, yet the moment she opened her front door, the fragrance of flowers—of freesias—assailed her.

She had always been susceptible to the memories evoked by scents. A whiff of Chanel No.5 brought her mother to mind as vividly as if she sat next to her in the quiet living room. A good Cuban cigar took her back to childhood, and Aspen at Christmas with Trish whose father lit up after dinner, and filled the house with the rich smell of expensive tobacco.

And now the intoxicating perfume of freesias swept over her in waves and brought Benedict alive in her mind more thoroughly than if he'd been standing there in person.

Dazed, she walked into her living room and found it full of flowers. Of freesias in glorious shades of purple and burgundy and yellow, in vases on the mantelpiece, and the coffee table. On the window ledges and the desk. Then, belatedly, she realized other things: the music coming from her stereo—songs from the forties about lost love found again, and two hearts beating as one; the windows open to the soft evening air; the aroma of bread warming in the oven.

As if drawn by invisible threads, she wandered through the other rooms. Came upon more freesias in the bedroom, and a sinfully seductive nightgown laid out on the bed. Discovered candles burning in her bathroom.

Finally, with her pulse fluttering and her spirit caught midway between hope and despair, she made her way to the terrace where she found the glass patio table set for dinner for two—and Benedict.

"Welcome home, *mi adorata*," he said, his voice embracing her like velvet.

"This is not possible!" she exclaimed, clutching the edge of the French door for fear she might faint with shock. "You're not really here!"

To prove her wrong, he came to her and swept her into his arms, and the feel of them closing firmly around her was very real indeed. "I am here," he said, "because this is where I belong. With you, my *bella* wife. Always with you."

"No," she protested, struggling to free herself because the temptation to forgive him was too overpowering to resist, and she knew she shouldn't give in to it. "You didn't meet me in Milan. You didn't keep your word."

"No," he admitted, releasing her just far enough that he could look into her eyes. "I did not, and for that I will always be sorry. But if you'll let me explain, perhaps you'll find it in yourself to forgive me one more time."

"I don't know that I can," she said, but allowed him to draw her down beside him on the padded cushions of the love seat under the eaves.

"Then at least agree to listen, before you pass judgment."

Well, she could hardly refuse to do that. And in all truth, as her shock dissipated, she found herself agog with curiosity. "How long have you been here?" she asked, sinking against him despite her best intentions to remain at a distance. "When did you have time to go to all this trouble?" Then, as another thought occurred,

"And how did you get inside my house? You don't have a key!"

"But Trish does," he said. "And Trish is a true romantic. Thank her for setting the scene, and thank me for having enough sense to turn to her when I needed help. Otherwise, you'd have found me sitting on the doorstep when you came home."

"But why, Benedict? Why put me through so much needless heartbreak?"

"Because I had no choice," he said, and told her the whole story.

"You could have phoned and warned me," she said, when he was done.

"And said what? That I was putting my mother ahead of my wife yet again, after promising it would never happen again? Should I have preyed on your sense of decency and fair play to blackmail you into staying in Italy when you were desperate to come home?" He shook his head. "No, it was better to tell you everything *after* the fact, when we were together again. Unfortunately, I arrived too late to make that happen in Milano, but I did my best, *cara*. I missed you by only a few minutes, and for the rest of my life, I will regret what that must have cost you."

She looked at him and saw that she was not the only one who'd suffered. Indeed, to be fair, he'd paid by far the greater price. Worry and exhaustion were painted on his face in equal measure.

"Well?" He returned her glance candidly, ready to accept whatever decision she meted out to him.

All her anger and pain dissolved. Overwhelmed, she pulled his head down to her breast and stroked her fingers through his hair. "You did what you had to do, my darling," she said softly. "And you're not the only one with regrets. As your wife, I should have been there to help you through such a very difficult time. I know how much it hurts to lose a mother. For your sake, I hope Elvira makes a good recovery.''

"I hope so, too. I would like you to know her as she used to be, instead of as she was these last few months. But what matters most is that you and I are together again.'' A tremor shook him. "I could not face losing you, Cassandra. You are more than my wife, you are my life.''

Courtesy of Trish, there was crab fresh from Fisherman's Wharf for dinner, and sourdough bread, and salad, and delicious little pastry shells filled with fresh strawberries. But it all had to wait until much later, when the moon had risen and the air had turned too cool to eat outdoors. Because there was more important business needing attention, and that took place in the bedroom.

"*Te amo*, Cassandra,'' he said, after they'd made love with the quiet intensity of two people who'd come too close to losing everything that mattered to them.

"*Te amo*, Benedict,'' she replied, lifting her face for his kiss.

November, four months later.

Even from the road, it was plain to see that the Constantino property was well-cared for, that order had been restored. The orchards stood lush with fruit. Huge padded baskets hung from the tree branches, slowly being filled with the precious hand-picked harvest of bergamot.

At the palazzo, a different Elvira waited. Still chic and sophisticated, still loving her ornately formal home, but with a softer edge to her voice, a warm albeit nervous welcome in her smile.

"I've brought your grandson to meet you," Cassie said, placing Michael Vincenzo in her mother-in-law's arms. "He is so much a Constantino that I think it's time the two of you met."

"Grazie," she replied, clearly on the verge of tears. *"Grazie tante,* Cassandra. It is more than I deserve. They tell me I treated you very poorly, *cara.* I hope you'll allow me to make it up to you and embrace you into my family as you deserve."

With a warmth she'd never have thought possible six months ago, Cassie enveloped both her son and his grandmother in a swift hug. "Of course! We all deserve nothing but good things from here on, Elvira. I'm very happy to see you looking so well."

"And I," she said, regaining her composure with difficulty, "am so grateful to you. I have only to look at my son to know that you are a good wife who makes him very happy, and to look at your son to know that you are also a very good mother. So, now we will go into the house. The rest of the family is anxious to meet this little one, and Speranza has been preparing for his visit for days."

Crooning softly to the baby, she led the way through the cavernous front hall to the salon at the back of the palazzo. Yet somehow, the gloom of the place seemed less oppressive, the cold of the ancient stone less pervasive.

Perhaps it had to do with Benedict's arm around her waist, and the secure knowledge that he would always be there, whether or not she needed him. Or perhaps it was much simpler than that, and merely had everything to do with love.

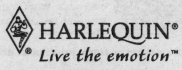

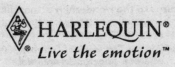

Like a phantom in the night comes
a new promotion from

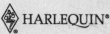
HARLEQUIN®

INTRIGUE®

GOTHIC ROMANCE

Beginning in August 2004, we offer you
a classic blend of chilling suspense and
electrifying romance, starting with....

A DANGEROUS INHERITANCE
LEONA KARR

And don't miss a spine-tingling Eclipse tale each month!

September 2004
MIDNIGHT ISLAND SANCTUARY
SUSAN PETERSON

October 2004
THE LEGACY OF CROFT CASTLE
JEAN BARRETT

November 2004
THE MAN FROM FALCON RIDGE
RITA HERRON

December 2004
EDEN'S SHADOW
JENNA RYAN

Available wherever Harlequin books are sold.
www.eHarlequin.com

HIECLIPSE

The world's bestselling romance series.

HARLEQUIN®
Presents

Seduction and Passion Guaranteed!

THE PRINCESS BRIDES

For duty, for money...for passion!

Discover a thrilling new trilogy from a rising star of Harlequin Presents®, Jane Porter!

Meet the Royals...

Chantal, Nicolette and Joelle are members of the blue-blooded Ducasse family. Step inside their sophisticated and glamorous world and watch as these beautiful princesses find they have to marry three international playboys—for duty, for money... and definitely for passion!

Don't miss

THE SULTAN'S BOUGHT BRIDE (#2418)
September 2004

THE GREEK'S ROYAL MISTRESS (#2424)
October 2004

THE ITALIAN'S VIRGIN PRINCESS (#2430)
November 2004

Pick up a Harlequin Presents® novel and you will enter a world of spine-tingling passion and provocative, tantalizing romance!

Available wherever Harlequin books are sold.

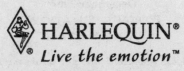

HARLEQUIN®
Live the emotion™

www.eHarlequin.com